WORKING FOR USPS

MY EXPERIENCE AS A CCA
(CITY CARRIER ASSISITANT)

A. GREGORY

WORKING FOR USPS

Prologue

Most of us in America don't really give much thought to our mail. We drop a letter in a mailbox, and basically just 'expect' it to arrive halfway across the country in a few days.

It's like magic in a way.

But guess what, folks. It's not magic, and though there are countless people other than the letter carriers that contribute to how our mail arrives to our door everyday, to me, from personal experience doing it, it's the actual letter carrier that is the backbone of the U.S. mail system.

But I have to go one step more with this evaluation. Though there are many part-time carriers that do a great job too, it is truly the full time ones, the ones who have ten and even twenty years in, that are the only reason any of us normal Joes out there in the country get our mail at all.

I have a family member who is a carrier, and for over fifteen years I have heard stories of how hard the job is, and the things that went on daily.

Of course I would sympathize, but not knowing the full range of the job, I could only nod and say how that sounded terrible when each situation was explained to me.

And then, in December 2015, I decided to give it a try myself. Now, I could have done many other things from past careers in my life if I wanted to re-enter the workforce. I could have found a job as either a line cook or as an apprentice culinary chef, both positions I held after leaving the U.S. Navy, where I was an MS, which is the name for a cook. On a submarine out of Groton, CT, a fast attack nuclear one at that, I would bake bread from scratch, dinner rolls too, bake pastries also from scratch, prepare sauces and the list goes on and on, serving an average of one hundred and fifty men on the sub, to over five thousand when working on the base itself.

I also could have gone back to driving professionally. I hold a class B CDL, which allows me to drive those large Greyhound busses you see all the time, and did a stint as a school bus driver (Note: when you see those red lights flashing on a school bus…STOP driving and don't pass it. You would be amazed how many don't.) Years ago I also drove around Boston for Old Town trolley, while giving tours of the city. Or I could use the CDL to drive a garbage truck, or maybe even get a job at the T, which here in Boston, Ma, is our public transit system. They always need qualified bus drivers.

Or I could have tried to refocus on my writing. Though books are in a depression if you're published in a small press, as kindle and self-publishing is slowly killing little presses, you never know when the next book written will be the one to 'put you on the map.'

Also, I was importing and then re-selling products through a third party website, but it rather fell apart, but I could have refocused my attentions there, and got back up and running through a different website. In a three month period I would usually pack and ship around three thousand packages all across the United States. It was a full time job in every way but without a time clock.

Now, I didn't just tell you all about my past adventures because I'm pontificating, (as I will leave that act to the manager of the postal station I was assigned to) but I simply needed to set the stage for the next part of this act.

See, if I'm correct—and I hope I am—you'll now at least give me the benefit of the doubt that I'm a rather intelligent person who has made a few accomplishments in his, well, let's call it the *resume of life.*

See, I need to get that established, so that later, when I'm telling you how complicated being a CCA was, or how difficult doing something was, as I went through CCA training and got on the street, you'll have a general idea of how intelligent I am—of course there's others who would beg to differ on that, but that's because they know me personally. (Wink, wink).

Okay, where was I? I got off track. See, there's so much to tell you in this book. There's so much I want to share. I was so blown away by the way it's all run, the incompetence at the higher levels and the magnificent competence at the letter carrier level.

Okay, I have it now.

The reason I took the job.

Well, that's a simple one.

It was easy to get hired; almost too easy really.

In fact, I have never found a job so easy to get accepted to in my entire life. Even McDonalds was a little tougher back when I tried years ago as a teenager—or so it seemed.

See, it appears that if you can pass a drug test, have a valid driver's license, and can clear a background check (like no felonies on that check) you're hired, just like that.

Employment history?

None needed.

Experience?

Hell no.

Have not a modicum of common sense and in a less political world would be categorized as mentally retarded?

Welcome aboard, and in fact for the last one, they might make you a supervisor or a manager.

But you gotta have a heartbeat. This seems to be a prerequisite. Oh, and you gotta be naïve as to what you're getting yourself into as a new letter carrier.

The ratio seems from my investigating that for every ten CCAs hired, three make it past the ninety days and stick around longer.

Oh, have I mentioned the ninety days, yet?

Well, like in most jobs, within ninety days, the employer (USPS) can 'can' your butt at a moment's notice. This weight is dangled over your head from the second you enter orientation. But trust me when I tell you don't worry about it, and really; don't even give it a second thought. Because later, once you arrive at your assigned station, you'll realize that USPS is so short of manpower that as long as you don't steal anything from the mail, the odds of you being terminated are pretty astronomical—and even then you might not get fired.

Case in point. Just after I finished writing this book, a CCA was caught throwing out mail so he didn't have to deliver it. He did not get fired immediately, and last I heard was still employed. See, throwing out mail still isn't 'stealing' it. So if you're wondering where that birthday card from Grandma is, you probably had that CCA as a letter carrier for a while.

So if you want the job, don't steal anything and don't let your LLV postal truck go rolling down the street by itself. (I will get into that more later.)

But though you didn't hear it from me, anything else you do while on the job is pretty much fair game.

Now of course, my experience was from working in only one IMC (station) and there are hundreds out there, but though not a gambling man, I would be surprised if most of the larger ones are not similar, though personalities would change depending on the person. The station I was in delivered to five or six cities, depending on if you add that number by individual city or zip codes (some cities have three zip codes).

Now that family member I told you about likes her station, and when I shared many anecdotes of my adventures she was pretty surprised, stating that those things would never happen in her place of operation. Also, I am in no way trying to trash the USPS. Despite the flaws I detail here, most of the men and women of the Postal Service do an amazing job of moving literally thousands of packages per day, millions per year. But if you are a fly on the wall in the locker room or break room, you'll find out that most of the letter carriers are overworked to the point of exhaustion, and many consider quitting each day from the sheer frustration, despite liking their job as a whole.

But the absolute contrast of what new employees are told in orientation (that is, that if the info was correct, it would make it a very safe and pretty nice place to work, despite the volume of mail), and what is actually going on (at this particular IMC anyway I went to) is so unbelievably maddening that I had to write about it.

So whether you want to know the real-world reality of how your postal system works in most large stations, or what it really is like being a letter carrier at one of them, then I hope you'll keep reading.

Because I believe there is one thing I can promise you in this book, and that's whether you're a regular citizen or have been in the USPS employ for years as a letter carrier.

I think you will find this all amusing and informative, and eye-opening.

Chapter 1
Drowning in Mail

The United States Postal Service is literally drowning in mail. The analogy goes like this. A man is drowning because he can't swim, but he keeps managing to push his face clear of the surface, to then suck in one more breath of air. But then he goes back down, the water closing over his head. Then, with a burst of energy, he thrusts out of the water again, once more sucking in that wonderful, life-giving air.

Only, as I said, he can't swim, so once more he goes under. So the question is: how long can he keep this up before he drowns and slowly floats to the bottom of the ocean?

This is the quandary of USPS, and at the moment, not only is not getting better, it's in fact becoming worse. The new analogy being that the drowning man now is attached to a cement block tied to his leg. Good luck, buddy, say hello to the fishes for me.

Five or six years ago I took the postal exam to be a letter carrier. I even passed, I'm proud to say. The exam score was good for two years from the day you're notified, so within that two years you need to be called to come in for an interview and get the process moving.

But here's the funny thing. Though the Union required in the contract with USPS that they had to give the test, the postal service was not hiring anyone.

Yes, that's right, they had a job freeze.

Now, this all goes back to what you've been hearing over the past few years, that the U.S. post office is going broke. Well, what we've all been told is completely wrong and misleading, but they have been dealing with some tough issues.

The largest issue is that Congress has dictated that the USPS (the only company in the entire U.S. to have to do this) must fund health benefits for up to seventy-five years into the future. That means they are forced to pay into a fund to have those benefits ready for people that aren't even born yet!

What company could basically throw out so much of their profits at the get-go? Well, despite this mandate, the U.S. post office is still showing a profit, and has been continually growing. Though letter mail is down drastically, packages are through the roof in volume.

The post office is also not funded by the government in any way, they are entirely self-sufficient when it comes to how they get their money. They get it like any business does: from their customers.

Years ago, the post office was doing so well that Congress said, "Okay, you're doing so good you don't need to be funded by us, so you're on your own." So much like a twenty-six year old getting kicked out of the house by his parents, (I mean, seriously, Jimmy, enough is enough, it's time to get your own place and let Mom and Dad have some time alone), so too did the post office become entirely in control of its profits.

But they were still hurting at this time, because of the future health benefits being funded. All their profits were going there, and there was nothing to run the entire system with. So they needed to start hacking and slashing their budget to make up all the money they were losing.

Okay, this is where it gets silly, and you wonder what happened to the people making these decisions, though by the end of this book, you'll probably assume they were promoted. See, some morons at the top of the ladder of command decided the number one thing costing them money were those pesky employees. What with the health benefits and vacations and sick time, plus having to pay them decent wages for the job, they needed to cut costs, and what could be better than stop hiring more people?

So for years there was a freeze on bringing in new employees full time, though there were more part time employees being added, for low wages and no chance to ever become full time, and zero benefits forever. USPS would hire them for ninety days, then basically fire them or lay them off, then rehire them. That was how they got around actually having to pay them benefits, vacation and sick days.

Oh, those clever bastards.

Okay, fast forward a few years, say to around 2013. Years have passed and suddenly many letter carriers and people in other positions in the postal service are reaching retirement age, and all of them are full time employees.

The full time ones (or *regulars* as they're called) are beginning to retire, and now there's no one to fill those positions.

But USPS isn't done digging a manpower hole it may take a decade to dig out of.

Amazon.com business is booming in online sales, and UPS the (Brown trucks) didn't fulfill their commitment to get all their parcels delivered on time for Christmas. Amazon isn't happy with UPS so they give the contract to USPS.

The high-ups think they can simply 'absorb' this new stream of millions of packages into the system, but in fact, this is the furthest thing from the truth. This is the classic example of the people in charge having no fucking clue what it's really like on the ground, doing the job day to day.

This is where the letter carriers Union stepped in, for if USPS goes down the toilet, then all their members are out of a job and let's face it, to have a Union, you gotta have people working to pay those Union dues.

The Union was able to add to the contact a new employee title. CCA.

Which stands for City Carrier Assistant. Those three letters make me cringe after doing it till I'd had enough.

The position has one positive. If you last a year or a little longer depending on what station you're at, all those retirees are leaving openings that CCAs can get in to. Once you become *regular* (remember that term?) you are then eligible for four weeks vacation a year, sick days and a retirement plan. Of course, that's if you live that long. Joking, but seriously, the job is slowly killing everyone who does it, even if they don't know it. Back problems, knee problems and more, the job really takes a toll on the people who do it.

From my vantage point of someone who knows a little more about the way it all works thanks to a family member, the whole 'making regular' thing is nothing more than a carrot dangled before a horse to keep it working. There are stations where five years later, you're still a CCA, with no extras to show for it. As of now, the pay is about sixteen dollars an hour. You can get ten or more working at Burger King or Target, so unless every single penny counts for you and you don't care how hard you work, the job is truly not worth it for most people, which is why seven out of ten leave fairly quickly.

And even when you stick it out and make regular, your pay only goes up fifty cents or so; there is no large jump when going from CCA to regular, though there are more benefits, such as sick time.

So when you meet someone delivering your mail and they say they're a CCA, you need to thank them for their hard work, because if the average citizen did the job for even a few hours, they would never look at their mailman the same way again. The gratitude and respect we owe these hardworking men and women is simply unbelievable, but there's no way to understand it all unless you walk a mile in their shoes—and if it's Headliner day it's even worse! (I'll get what those are in another chapter.)

Still don't believe how much what those letter carriers do matters to us all?

In the next chapter, I'll explain how incredibly important USPS was to the stability of our country in the past, and still is today—something I didn't know until seeing it for myself.

Chapter 2
On Strike!

Before 1970, letter carriers were working for three dollars an hour, didn't have an eight hour work week, benefits, or any of the things most of us expect when we work practically anywhere nowadays, and though the Union fought for better conditions and wages, all decisions for USPS had to be decided by Congress. And we all know how well that works when we really want to get something done.

Back then, a letter carrier would have to wait twenty-one years before reaching the top step of their pay grade level. That meant if you started at three dollars an hour and the most you could get was seven, it would take twenty-one years worth of raises before you could get paid that higher amount.

But in March 1970, after Nixon deferred a promised wage increase, the carriers in New York had had enough, and though it was stated in their contract that they couldn't strike, they did anyway, feeling there was nothing left to lose.

Like wildfire other states across America joined in, and soon all across the country, from large cities to small towns, numbering over 200,000, the strikers stood firm.

Immediately, court orders were issued demanding the letter carriers get back to work, and many workers found themselves hiding from federal process servers. These men were risking jail time and the loss of their jobs! Without their jobs how would they pay their bills, survive? They had families counting on their salaries, no matter how small it was at the time.

But much like in any revolution, it takes brave souls, people willing to risk it all, to make changes in society and government.

With no one delivering the mail, and a time way before email and cell phones, the country literally came to a screeching halt. Wall Street had to shut down. In the '70s if someone needed notification of an important meeting, letters would be mailed. When no one could get mail, suddenly documents were frozen, for who is going to fly across the country to get a document signed when it could be delivered by the post office for what is even now, an incredibly affordable price?

Nixon, knowing the mail needed to keep moving, brought in 25,000 soldiers to replace the striking carriers, but when setting up a *route*—which is the collection of streets and buildings in a given area—to walk in blindly would mean a job that took a skilled letter carrier an hour, would take half a day for a novice to complete. And once on the street delivering mail, if the person was unfamiliar with the area, it would take even more time to complete the route, something a knowledgeable letter carrier would do in a fraction of the time.

And this is taking account that with letter carriers on strike across the country, little mail was reaching the stations before it could be sorted.

Magazines such as Newsweek and Time had covers dedicated to the strike. Titles such as **"The Day the Mail Stopped!"** and simply **"Strike!"** were splattered across newsstands.

But with the soldiers called in mostly ineffective due to their lack of skill in the job, eight days after it began, the Union and Congress came to an agreement and the strike was over, the men returning to work.

When they returned, they received amnesty for striking, better wages with better raises at given times, benefits, and better hours.

But one other important thing came out of all this as well.

Where before the strike, all decisions for USPS went through Congress, one of the reforms was for the post office to become independent of Congress when it came to making decisions, which meant the Union could now negotiate more effectively with USPS.

You can imagine the feeling of coming back to work after the strike, the joy the men felt for not only getting back to work, but for the better conditions and wages.

But what meant even more than the better wages and benefits, was the new sense of dignity each employee had. For when you're paid what you deserve to do a job, you feel valued, that your contribution matters, and one way that can be shown is by how much you're paid for the task you're completing.

The strike of 1970 is so much more than men seeking better wages and benefits. To me, it signifies everything that makes our country great. That when we as a people have had enough, are tired of being taken advantage of, that we can stand up and scream: "No more!" and wield enough influence to make Congress fall to their knees and negotiate, when they believed they had all the power.

In the end, we the people of this great country are its backbone, not Congress, or the government itself. We are the ones who get up day to day, go to work, pay our bills, buy groceries, start small business and pay our taxes.

Without us, this country is nothing, and together we can do anything and everything.

So whether you're a fan of the Union or not is irrelevant. This isn't a story about the Union, it's a tale about the dignity of the American worker, and how we will not allow ourselves to be trampled under the foot of corporate greed.

We all owe the men who went on strike more than four decades ago a debt of gratitude, and each day, when a letter or a package is left at a doorstep or placed in a mailbox, what those men did reverberates through the years, to this very day.

Chapter 3
Applications, Tests And Background Checks

Like I explained in a previous chapter, from talking to letter carriers who have been around for years, I know that if you have a few things lined up in your resume, such as a valid drivers license for one year, can pass a background check (no felonies), a drug test, and know how to read and write, you're pretty much guaranteed a job as a CCA.

So I figured what the hell, why not find out how hard this job is first-hand, for there's no way to truly know someone else's job unless you walk a mile in their shoes—or five miles or more daily, as the case may be sometimes.

Okay, so here's the step by step to how you go through the process.

First, you go to the USPS website and make a profile. Anyone with basic computer skills should be able to do this. They ask the usual information you would expect.

When it comes to the 'job history' part, don't panic. Either put every job you've had for the past ten years or simply tell them you've been unemployed. Or better yet, have some fun and tell them you've been in Africa building schools and churches. It won't matter—they don't care!

They need warm bodies, and with the exception of a few prerequisites, everyone gets hired!

Now I have to share something here. I think delivering the mail is an honor, one of the oldest pastimes in our country, and to do the job well, I would think you would need to be rather intelligent, but to become a CCA, this is not even relevant, though almost all of the people I met were in fact very intelligent and hardworking.

The ones that weren't were usually in supervisor or management positions—not all but some of them.

If you think delivering the mail is easy, I'll explain further in other chapters how this is so far from the truth it's off the map. The concept may be simple, however the actual process is pretty difficult and overly complicated.

Okay, so you've made a profile on the USPS website. Now you get to see what fun jobs are available.

When you go on the site, you may see a few other jobs for CCA, but you'll also see A LOT, and I mean A LOT of openings for CCAs. At the time of writing this book, they needed literally hundreds of bodies thanks to the job freeze for so long, and because they now have new accounts such as Amazon; so the amount of packages to be delivered daily has tripled, only there's no new manpower to move the mail.

But I'm getting ahead of myself again.

Okay, so you're seeing CCA as a position to pick. On the site, there'll be different locations besides each CCA job. Be warned now. Let's say you live on the north side of Boston, so you pick on the north side to be close, but still, you could end up driving to an annex (or station) within a sixty mile radius, and with cities such as Boston and Cambridge being what they are, even a fifteen mile commute could take over an hour of stop-and-go traffic.

But none of that may matter to you, as you need a job that pays well, and a CCA position offers sixteen dollars an hour. Right now, you don't see the work ahead, you only see five dollars more an hour than if you worked at a super market or superstore like Target or Walmart.

Still, sometimes you get lucky and they'll assign you close to home by your home zip code. Since writing this book, I hear they are trying even more to keep you closer to home.

I was placed in a large IMC in Chelsea, Ma. Though some stations only have two or even one city to deliver to, the one I was assigned to had five or six cities, and one city called Somerville had three zip codes, which says how truly large the city is. This was one of the largest annexes in all of Massachusetts.

Still, once you pick your choice location on the website, you have to cross your fingers that you don't get screwed on where they send you.

By the way, I want to talk about this a little more for a second.

When you go to say Target, or even apply for a job at the countless businesses in Boston, you pick said job sometimes by its location to where you live. Though many people travel to work, others have found out that even if you took a pay cut or lost seniority, to have a travel time of fifteen or twenty minutes to work, over say, an hour, each day, adds to the quality of your life, and that the cut in pay or perks isn't an issue overall.

What this means for you is that if you get your assignment and its pretty damn far from where you live as a commute, simply turn them down. You'll then just quickly go through the process again, and hopefully this time will get a station closer to home. Trust me here, please, this is fact. They need bodies so bad it's painful to see. They will quickly run you through the process again, and this time you might get a better location.

Still, I wasn't pleased with any of this, but as I wasn't desperate for this job, I had nothing to lose. If I had been assigned to say Cambridge, from where I live, which is a terrible commute, I wouldn't have accepted the job. But I got lucky and I was fifteen minutes from home. Oh, lucky me.

Anyway, after you pick your location, the next step is going to be that you take a test online. I found this amusing because anyone could take it for you. I could have asked my son to do it for me, if I didn't want to bother. The test is simple, where they ask moral questions and you need to decide what they want to hear.

One example that was not on the test (as I can not legally talk about the test) that was similar would be that if you saw someone stealing, would you tell a supervisor?

Now, I would think yes, you would, and I hope you do, too, but if you did say 'yes,' would they consider you a snitch for doing so? Or would they really want you to say yes.

It's really a psychological test and is absolutely ridiculous for the position you're taking. As it's given online with no way to supervise the applicant, I highly doubt what you put matters, unless you always say the exact opposite of what a common sense person might put for an answer.

But still, if asked what you would do if someone was stealing or doing something wrong, (not saying this is on the test, just a hypothetical of course) I would go with telling a supervisor. But in reality, with the way the system works within USPS, I would keep my mouth shut and mind my own business, unless you have truly great people as your leaders. This can happen but unfortunately not too often. They say that those that can, do, and those that can't, become management. This is a practice put into effect every day at USPS. Sad but true. Not all the time but more times than not.

Okay, so you've taken the psych test you're required to take at home, and with the test taken by you, or you had someone do it for you, either way, it's done.

That's pretty much it. If I missed something it will be small and the step-by-step process when you take the test will walk you through it.

Now, besides the stuff you did on your home computer to apply, you're going to have to do some running around on your own time if you want this job.

One trip will be to a doctor's office picked from a list close to your home, where you will get to pee in a cup so that USPS can be sure you're not on crack, heroin or any other drugs. Once you have this test and are hired, you'll probably never get another drug test. So if you like such things, first to clean out your system, drink pickle juice or some such nonsense, and if you pass the test, you can then go nuts again if that's what you want. Now, while this is going on, behind the scenes, you'll be getting a background check. I was told they only go back ten years, so if you were tied to a plot to blow up the White House or were involved with a terrorist cell fifteen years ago, you should be okay. But don't take my word for it. Well, maybe those aren't good examples, but I think you get my meaning. If you don't, that's okay, too, that means you're probably a perfect candidate to being a CCA.

I want to also mention that I began this odyssey around the end of the year at the end of the month, and for me, because I dragged my heels on replying to emails they sent, It took me around thirty days to arrive for Orientation, so you can get an idea how long it takes.

Now there's a form you are going to need to print out for your background check. The form had some confusing information, such as not all people needed to send it. Knowing the government (USPS is government) has a way about them, I decided to send it anyway, to make sure there was no way to screw the application up. Now, get this; you need to fax it to a place in South Carolina or some state around there.

Fax it? Seriously? Is that even a thing anymore? I thought people simply scanned documents and emailed them nowadays?

So I had to find a fax machine, and luckily I know someone who worked in an office that would let me use it.

I get there, we try to fax it, and it gets rejected. We tried for over an hour around lunchtime and no go, it won't go through. I was frustrated. I needed to get this there. Did the place have only one fax machine? There's only one number to use. This place does background checks for the entire USPS, and other companies as well, I assume. And they have one single fax machine? Seriously?

I quickly imagined a broom closet, with the name of the closet crossed out and a piece of paper hanging at an odd angle saying the name of this company. Inside was a small desk with a phone book holding up one leg. On the desk is simply a laptop and calendar, and on the wall of the four-by-four room, is a poster of a cat hanging from a tree limb. The words: "Hang in there!" printed in cheerful font.

Made me think back to when I took that Assessment Exam (will talk about that in a moment), the rented suite room, the word 'suite' just a fancy term for using what room was empty and could be rented, where the scotch tape from previous renters isn't even bothered to be removed, and the faded outlines of where pictures hung on the walls from past renters is prevalent.

Well, what did I expect?

There was an address so I mailed it, then figured I would keep trying to fax it. See, you get five days for them to get it, so you have to be prompt.

But the fax never went through, despite my friend trying for the rest of the day on my behalf.

I told my family member who was a letter carrier and they took it to work and had their supervisor try for me at six A.M. the next morning. Then it went through, luckily.

Still, why was this so needlessly complicated?

Easy; it has to do with the U.S. Post Office. Get used to it if you want to work for them.

* * *

Okay, so you passed the background check and no one has arrived at your door with a search warrant because you flunked the drug test.

The next item you need to do on your own time is go to a facility near you and take another test.

But I need to elaborate on this.

It's not a test.

Not even close.

It's an Assessment Exam.

Say it with me. A-ss-ess-ment Ex-am.

Nowhere in that title is the word test.

You know why? Because it's not a test!

USPS just wants to know if you have a fourth grade education or higher.

Now, I'm not gonna talk about the exam in detail because I vaguely remember clicking a button about privacy or something. Like most of us, when I see blah, blah, blah, agree, with words so small you would need the Hubble telescope to read them, I usually just click *agree*. Still, I agreed and I'm a man of my word, and I won't give USPS an excuse to go after me. When this book is released and if word gets out, I doubt they'll be too happy about it. I say, "Tough! This is America and it's my right to free speech as stated in the Constitution."

But though I won't talk about the actual exam, I will share a few things I found amusing and relevant to my entire experience.

So I arrive at the suite, which was a room rented in an office building. There's this guy wearing headphones on his head watching a movie on his laptop.

I walk in and you can feel the chill coming off this guy. To him, you're just another face; he's not there to so much as agree that the weather is okay outside, and just wants to prop you before your 1990's monitor and get back to his action movie he's watching on his laptop. He walks me into a second room where there are about twenty monitors so big you could kill someone with one of you dropped it on them.

You'll see this a lot with USPS. Twentieth century technology that is state-of-the-art, mixed in with hardware right out of the 1970s and 80's. (During orientation a phone rang, one of those ring tones from a 1970's phone, what with the large receiver and square box with a rotary wheel to dial. When I heard the ring I assumed it was one of the applicant's cell phones, and how it's funny and ironic to place that ring tone on a modern cell phone. So I was pretty amazed when the instructor walks over to a small table in the corner of the room to an actual phone made in the 70's and answers it.)

There were a couple of other people taking the test as well when I arrived, and the 'custodian of the fabled monitors' sets it up and off I go.

Now once more, I'm not going to talk about the test, but trust me, If you can read and write, you won't have any trouble.

But what I will share, to allay any feelings of nervousness when you take the test is that on one part I missed a full twenty questions and at the end of the test, in a different section, I was so aggravated with my previous mistake, and assumed I had already failed, that I simply placed the letter 'B' for each consecutive answer of multiple choice for the hell of it, figuring it didn't matter anyway.

I left the building feeling terrible. My ego had just taken a terrible hit. I mean, most of us have an idea when we take a test if we failed or passed, right?

Well, from talking to other letter carriers, and hearing about some of the CCAs that had been hired and their skill levels, I was pretty downtrodden on my own skills as a human being. I'd heard that if those people could get hired, well for myself then, with what I feel is rather decent intelligence, I should have had no problem at all!

Hah! If that was so true, why did I miss twenty answers and fail when the clock for that section ran out?

I quickly had to tell myself I was either too smart or too dumb to get this job, which consoled some of my dejected feelings, but not much.

In a way it was good. We as human beings can get a little too big for our britches and it's good sometimes to be brought back down to earth.

Well, no sooner did I leave the building than I got an email with my test scores, but I needed a lap top to access the data so I sulked all the way home.

But I forgot one important thing that now you will know and remember, that I already stated at the beginning of this chapter.

This was not a test, it was never a test; it was an 'assessment' exam.

And I think it's set up on such a sliding scale that even an unintelligent person will probably pass.

How do I know this?

Because I practically fell out of my chair when I opened the file and saw that I had received a seventy-three for a test score.

What! A seventy-three!

I must have done pretty damn good on what I did answer, and I guess all those letter B's must have been correct rather than not.

So I had passed the test and was on my way to being accepted for the job.

The only other thing to mention for this part of getting the job is that you'll get emails at most stages of the process. In the emails they give you seven days to reply. Now, seems I was applying in November, and I sure as hell didn't want to start during Christmas, I waited until day six each time I received an email to drag the process out. I figured if you click on them immediately, less than a month will pass before you're stepping onto the job site.

Okay, so if you've jumped through all the hoops I've stated above and passed each one, you're in.

You'll get an actual phone call now, the first real person you'll have spoken to since applying, where you'll simply be confirming whether you still want the job and told where to go for Orientation. (If you live within sixty miles of Boston, you'll go to the main building in Boston on Dorchester St, behind South Station, which is where I went. So if you live on the Cape, or an hour west of Boston, get ready for a week long commute into the city.

About a week later or so after the phone call, you'll get an email telling you where your assignment will be. But be warned, there are times where districts are entirely separate from others. I will give you an example in the Boston area. The city of Cambridge is its own entity, so if you were in Cambridge and ten years later decided you'd had enough of the long commute, as two hours round trip was cutting into family time when added to the ten or eleven hours you were working each day, and you wanted to transfer to another office, you'd lose all your seniority in that new office as far as bidding on routes, when you get to take your vacation, ect. Everyone would be above you. You'd still have your time in as far as pay and benefits, but all the other stuff would put you at the bottom of the list.

Seniority is everything in the post office. USPS, along with the Union, makes working there like a clubhouse for kids, where the longest members get the most perks. Its great if you've been around for a while, but if you're new, you get nothing and have no say and are basically fu…I mean screwed. You will never get vacation in the summertime, never get to put in for a Saturday off, because senior guys use their vacation days as fast as they can get them. Why? Because they're burnt out and want another day off as fast as possible. A lot of the older carriers near retirement are simply like old horses limping across the finish line so they can get more money for retirement when they finally leave, so they need to keep on going for a few more years, despite being exhausted and having had enough.

All this means that if you end up in one of those separate districts and you stay for a while, you'll quickly find yourself trapped there or else become low man on the totem pole at the new annex.

Most people won't transfer, as like I said earlier, seniority is paramount to attempting to have a life while working as either a CCA or a 'regular' letter carrier later on.

But though most won't ever do this, I wanted to mention one particular instance I know of where a regular carrier said "Enough, I'm tired of this commute." He transferred from Cambridge to Chelsea, where he cut his commute from over an hour to fifteen minutes. Upon meeting him, my first instinct was how nice and friendly he was. (This needs to be stated because later, I met people that I had an immediate dislike to and want to put it all into context. I like people, and love chatting with them, but there are times when you meet people that you just don't like. I'm sure people have felt that about me as well. Funny how we do that; sizing up personalities within seconds of meeting someone. A smile goes a long way on first meetings, I think.) But when that person you dislike ends up being someone of authority over you, it makes working in that environment even more difficult.

This carrier's wife works at the same annex, too, and when I met her, I have rarely met someone so sweet and cheerful, and she must be one tough woman to do the job as a mail carrier. The couple has a young child together and how they both work sixty-plus hours a week and juggle the child is truly one for the books.

So if you truly want to do this as a career, be careful where you go for your station, because the years pass too quickly to count and you might end up woefully regretting where you're now basically trapped.

And one more thing you need to know if you take this job—and for some this will be a positive, but others, you'll now want to run away screaming.

You'll be expected to work a mandatory sixty hours or more work week, with only one day off a week—if you're lucky. You will work Sundays.

As a CCA, you have no say in your hours. The post office is so hurting for help, they need you all the time. They aren't doing this because they want to slowly kill you, but because there's simply so much mail and packages that if they don't have everyone working a zillion hours, they'll become so buried that they'll never dig themselves out.

So if you're looking for a job with zero family time but lots of hours to work, you should be very happy here. You get overtime over an eight hour work day, not over forty per week. So work eight hours on Monday, then on Tuesday work ten hours, and for some reason you don't work the rest of the week, you still receive two hours of overtime for working Tuesday.

That's about all the consolation you'll get, though, and don't forget to thank the Union for fighting for that perk.

Pats on the back will be nonexistent in this job. Want someone to tell you that you did a good job today? Not going to happen. Your 'good job' is that they let you go home after an eleven hour work day, where it was raining cats and dogs the entire day.

So if you have some sort of life, family, friends, maybe a few hobbies; say goodbye to it all, because there's simply not enough time in the day. All your waking hours will now be spent working for USPS, and if you decide it's not working out, and wish you could work a little less, forget it, for your only option is to resign.

Chapter 4
Orientation: A Long And Boring Week

A letter carrier I know well, who has been working for USPS for over a decade, told me to enjoy Orientation, for it would be the easiest work I ever did for the post office—but he said I would be bored as hell.

In many ways he was totally correct, but in other ways he was wrong.

The first two days of Orientation is really all about the post office telling you this and that for the sole purpose of when you screw up later, they have documented proof that they told you, and because they did this, it's your fault whatever you did wrong.

Deniability in all its forms right here, all rolled up into two days of figureheads who have most definitely been drinking the Kool-aid.

If you don't know what that term means, I'll explain it.

In cults, such as one where the leader says everyone needs to die, so that their souls can float up to the Mother ship hovering in the atmosphere, so then they can all go to Alpha Centari or some other made-up planet, Kool-Aid is tainted with some sort of poison and the entire cult drinks it.

Mass suicide.

The endless faces that will drop in on those first two days, preach this and that, and all like to start their lectures with how long they've been working for USPS. All were well over ten and fifteen years and a few even had over twenty-plus.

They will all tell you how they carried mail at one time, but what they don't focus on in any way, is that most of them carried mail before the creation of the internet. Carrying mail now, compared to back when these guys carried, is a very different situation, what with the scans and bulk mail, and drowning in parcels.

But they desperately want to get that out there, so that later, when you may be feeling overwhelmed, you're supposed to remember that all those guys did it; so why can't you?

I truly wonder; if most of them received a demotion for some reason, and had to go out again and become a letter carrier once more, with no other options other than to leave the job, just how great they would do now, how much they would love their job. I'm sure some would do it of course, but I would be truly surprised if most didn't fail miserably.

With the exception of one or two people, almost every person dropping by to chat was overweight and one or two would be considered 'grossly' overweight.

You're going to hear a lot of anecdotes, stories from these people of what they saw happen while working over the years, or what they knew of and are now conveying to you. Most of these stories are rather entertaining, and thank God they're added to the curriculum. You'll quickly figure out that there's easily about six hours of actual information you're being given in the first two days, but it needs to be spread out over a two day, sixteen hour journey, so that USPS can say that at the end of the full week, you received a full forty hour week of training.

Once more, deniability for them. But if you mess up out there and can prove no one ever told you, supposedly you won't be responsible, so they make damn sure it's all told to you so they can hang you with it later.

Yes, that's right. Hang you right out to dry with the wet laundry. No, it's not put in those exact terms, but if you were like me and had someone you knew well already working as a letter carrier, and had prior military service and knew how the government works, it was entirely clear to me.

Now, I did my orientation around the last week of 2015, so in this particular week, a lot of people who would talk to the class went on vacation, so in many ways the people doing the orientation 'winged it' as now there was even more time to fill and no content to fill it with. There was no uniformity and because of this, there was a lot of repetition over the same subjects.

What ended up happening is one person would go through stuff in a booklet you received, filled with information and 'modules,' and later, a different person would go over the same thing just to fill time.

I quickly realized that the entire week of information was spoon-fed so that they expected the lowest of intelligence to understand. So be prepared to be bored out of your mind, but at the same time enjoy it, because later, when it's ten degrees out, and you have packages spilling onto your lap in your postal truck, and you're running two hours behind, you'll wish you were back in that nice warm classroom being bored to tears.

* * *

Another thing to note is there were break rooms with microwaves located around the building of the Orientation, and there should be one close to your classroom, so unless you want to use the cafeteria, which is fine, the food pretty affordable,(five bucks for a sub) you can bring your own lunch, heat it up and stay inside. Given that you get around thirty minutes for lunch, it's easier to do this, but some people don't take lunches, only buy them.

On one of the days, the Postal Police came to speak, warning you what they'll do to you if you steal or cross their paths.

We get back from lunch and there are these two officers standing in the corner, waiting for the class to begin.

Now, the first man is a little over six feet tall, with a fit physique and a commanding presence. His service revolver is on his hip and he's wearing a Kevlar vest over his dark-blue shirt. He has dark hair and a strong jaw. To me, he represented exactly what a police officer should look like, in whatever service he was working for.

But this man leaves as soon as we all sit down.

Now, the second officer looked very different from the first, and was the exact opposite of what I would expect to see of a policeman in general, although sad to say, he fit that stereotypical idea that people joke about. The best reference for most people to imagine this individual's size, and I'm not exaggerating here, was he was the living embodiment of Chief Wiggum from *The Simpsons* TV show.

My first impression was amazement; that this man was in the Postal Police. I mean, didn't they have some sort of physical fitness test each year? How did this man chase a suspect?

I assumed, if I was so bold to ask that question, I would have received the cavalier answer that he would simply shoot the suspect and then take his time reaching the poor guy—nod, nod, wink, wink, of course he wouldn't, but question deferred.

Grossly overweight was the only description.

But once the man introduced himself, I found he was a man to be respected, someone who was extremely intelligent and knew his job very well. If I needed help, I would be glad if this man showed up.

As long as I didn't need him to run to reach me, of course.

See, in the back of my mind, I couldn't get past the sheer size of this guy. It just wasn't what I expected, and for the rest of my short time as a CCA, not much was, which was why I ended up writing this book, and for other reasons as well that will be mentioned later.

Also, I wanted to add that if you're driving in for the orientation in Boston, you'll be allowed to park in a lot ten minutes or so walk from the building. An email will arrive with relevant information for how to do that. There's also a shuttle that goes back and forth, so if you do park in the lot, and you see the little kiosk that resembles what you see when waiting for a city bus, and see a van there, idling, that's for postal employees to take so you don't have to face the cold walk over the Summer St. bridge—in the winter it's brutal!

One other thing to add is I recommend bringing some snacks with you, which should be allowed inside the classroom. Not knowing when you might get a ten minute break, if you're stomach begins to ask for food, you may find the classroom intolerable.

I know when I'm doing a physical job, I don't mind being a little hungry. It even gives me an edge while working, but when sitting in a class for hours, and you begin to feel that familiar rumbling, if you don't satiate it, you'll find yourself becoming distracted, and the class will become more insufferable than before.

The classroom hours ran from around seven in the morning to three to three-thirty each day. If you're not used to sitting in a classroom setting, it'll take some getting used to. But once the first two days are over and you go into the rest, and the lecturers begin throwing form after form at you, you're going to long for the past two days, I promise.

Oh, and one more thing. Beware of conflicting information. Though they would never admit this, I found that a lot of these people that spoke were very out of touch with the day-to-day operations that went on within the actual annexes. So no matter what they say, I recommend taking it with a grain of salt and check on it yourself later. So if you hear something that concerns you, don't quit because what you heard upset you. It's probably not correct anyway, and a lot of these people should stick to the script given and not go off topic.

When we get to Chapter 7, you'll understand even more what I mean (And no peeking, read in order here, or it all won't make sense, though I assume the title of Chapter 7 says it all.)

Chapter 5
Forms, Forms And More Forms

Welcome to day three, the first of three days where you're not going to learn what you need at all for when you become a CCA for real.

The teacher I had was a man who was an actual letter carrier in his city, and he also trained new CCAs a few days a week. Like most people you'll meet, he had been carrying for many years and if there was one thing I got from the second he began speaking, was that he was damn good at his job.

This made me sit up and want to listen. Finally, someone who did the job and did it damn well, who was out there right now.

But this is where my own knowledge of how it really was out there working as a mail carrier from other carriers sharing with me, caused me immediate difficulty.

See, as the teacher talked, everything he said sounded wonderful, and if all he taught us was put into practice out there, by all the other carriers out there, USPS would truly be a wonderful place to work.

The only problem was that though maybe in his office these practices happened, or maybe he just had to teach us what he was told to, and what would really be expected of us would change from station to station, I quickly found myself rolling my eyes as we went from module to module.

Now hold on, before you think I'm being an ass, let me explain with one good example of what he was teaching and what was really going on when you're thrown to the wolves and have to actually do the job.

This can vary from station to station, but at least three letter carriers I know well, people I know that work out of annexes, when I asked them about this particular example, they all laughed and said it would never happen.

So, this is the example: There's a black, hardbound folder that's on each of the routes. Within this black folder should be all the information a new carrier would need before doing the route. You, as a CCA, getting assigned a route you've never delivered on before, would want to look inside this black folder. Here, all the joys of being a mail carrier are made easy for you, so you can be proactive and do a good job that day. Within this glorious folder, you'll find maps of the route, and relevant information about said route, such as what homes have *Holds* on them (means not getting mail), what homes don't get mail because the steps are damaged and it's not safe to deliver, and any other pertinent information before setting out on that route that day.

So from what you were taught in orientation, the black book will give you any and all information you need to get your route done.

So I go home for the day and ask my carrier friends about the black book. The reply was simply, and with a little sadness. "Yeah, they don't update those. Hell, I don't even know if there's one on my route?"

Still, maybe where I was going in Chelsea, it would be okay, after all, each station is different depending on who's running it. It shouldn't be this way but it is. So while doing training with letter carriers when I arrived in Chelsea, I asked them about the black book, and each time I received the same answer. "The book has nothing updated, it's not worth looking at."

Gee, what a surprise. So you go out and deliver blind, not knowing what important information you don't know.

But I'll get into more on that in later chapters, when I actually went out and delivered mail.

For the next three days of Orientation, you're going to be bombarded with forms. 1260s, 3849s, and a thousand others. There are countless pieces of equipment you're going to be taught, such as bins painted orange they call *pumpkins* and when you need to get keys you go to the *cage*, and on and on.

Yes, I could write most of it down right now from memory here, if I wanted to show off in some weird way, as what I didn't pick up in training, I already knew from years of dealing with either my online shipping business or from simply asking my friends who were letter carriers. I always ask questions, even to them before I began training. That's how you learn in this world after all.

But this is what I'm trying to get at, and like usual am taking forever to get to the point.

Though I was mostly familiar with more than half of the forms and pieces of equipment the day I began Orientation, even I felt overwhelmed with each new document. So if you aren't familiar with any of the documents, you're really going to feel overwhelmed.

I'll tell you this, and if there's one thing you should take with you from this book, take this: You don't need to know all the forms the day you start, and in fact will only use a handful on a daily basis. So don't go nuts when form after form is tossed out at you in class, because really it just won't matter. You'll learn as you go when you train with a few different letter carriers before they set you loose on your own.

Here's another example of forms you'll probably never need.

There's a form for C.O.D.s. Remember those? If you're over forty you might. Younger readers will have no idea.

Back before the internet, people would pay Cash On Delivery, paying their letter carrier to get their package. In class, the teacher spent about ten minutes or so discussing and teaching us how to fill out the form, one more form added to what will feel like hundreds, and though not as much as that, it'll come close.

In seventeen years, the family member I know as a letter carrier has had only one COD, and that was years ago. So you're basically learning a form you'll *never* use.

Another thing to remember is when the picture slides are being used by the teacher. Like most things in the post office, the slides are outdated, and new equipment is being used now, such as new scanners, new forms and a few miscellaneous items such as carts to move mail.

I would think the teacher would have skipped over these, as why would you teach a class about equipment and forms not in use anymore? But yup, though he did quickly say we didn't use those items anymore, he then went into a detailed explanation on what the form or equipments did and was used for. To him it was nothing, as he was incredibly experienced and knowledgeable, but to the class of new faces, for most of them from what I saw when I studied faces and chatted about this stuff later, it was more information being forced into an already full mind. That's the way I saw it. Why would you teach me how to drive a Ford Pinto if I drive a 2015 Buick everyday?

There was one man who sat in the back near me, and I constantly saw him shaking his head in frustration. When there were class breaks, I would explain that he didn't need to know half the stuff he was being taught at the beginning, and would learn all he needed to know while doing actual training. I don't know if it helped, but I tried to soothe his fears. He thought from day one he would have to know it all and it was frustrating him big time.

So relax when all the forms are being thrown at you. The class is really just to get you familiar with them, despite the fact they toss them all at you at once.

There are only a few forms and actions with the mail scanner that you'll use on a daily basis.

The most important are:

Certified: You need to get a signature, but trust me, it's simple. If the person isn't home, you scan the barcode on the peach form and leave it for the customer.

Registered Mail: Mostly same as above. This mail is kept in a locked cage to keep it safe, not in the general mail stream.

Signature Confirmation: Pretty much like Certified.

Express Mail: These are delivered by either twelve noon, three P.M. or by the end of the business day. You might get some on your route so do them first.

The form you'll use most of the time for all these deliveries is playfully called a 'peach puppy' (Form 3849), because it's peach colored. Many of you may have received one when you had a delivery and weren't home to accept the item and a signature was required. It's what you'd bring to the local post office to get your package or letter.

The only other thing you'll do on a daily basis other than delivering letters, magazines and junk mail, is deliver packages. And believe me, you will be delivering *a lot* of packages. Here you'll need to scan the item as *delivered* when leaving it. Once you do it a few times, you won't have a problem after that. The scanner isn't complicated for most people. The menu on what do to for packages is simple, too. Such as if you attempted to leave a package but didn't need a signature, you'd simply scan the package and then scroll down the page until you found the word 'attempted.' Click it and all done.

Though I found this odd when asking carriers I trained with, none of them even new how to *accept* an outgoing package if one was offered. So if someone sold something on eBay and purchased pre-paid postage, these carriers would just take it back to the station but not scan it as *Accepted*.

It goes to show that though these guys had been in for twenty years, where they delivered, mostly low income, no one ever shipped an item and used the mail carrier for a pickup. So though the word 'accepted' was clearly there on the menu, because they never, ever, did it, they didn't even know how.

So it was rather odd that I actually taught them what to do with the scanner and how a pickup like that works. (Before I took the job, a few letter carriers told me I was probably too smart for the job. Smart maybe, but mental fortitude I think I was woefully lacking. You need to turn off your brain to do this job and I'm someone who just can't do that.)

So to repeat one more time; don't freak out when all the forms are thrown at you, number after number of said forms recited, and when you're later brought to a different classroom, where they put you into a little cubicle where you'll learn to *throw* mail, don't get concerned.

Learning to sort mail on a route is simple memory. The first time you're told to do a particular route when at your station, and have never seen it before, it's going to be pretty tough, but after a few times, simple memory will let you do the job smoother. I found this part of the job easy, as if you can read, you can do this without even thinking. But more on that later when I get to the station and the real training begins.

Chapter 6
Around And Around We Go

Congratulations; you made it through Orientation.

Today is the day of your LLV training. The LLV is the short term for those little square postal vehicles you see letter carriers driving. Long Life Vehicles they call them.

Well, as I will tell you and you will find out for yourselves, if these vehicles have *long lives*, they used them up over a decade ago.

These vehicles are bare bones, and the heat barely works in them. No air conditioning and no radio. The window is a roll-crank, and the headlights have to be turned on by pulling out a knob. If you're over forty you'll know about this, as years ago headlights were separate from the electrical system and you manually turned them on and off.

Now, before you can drive one of these little gems, you're going to spend half a day during the week of Orientation going through driver safety class.

This may very well be the most grueling part of the entire week. The curriculum is at a third grade level and the videos are terrible—once more, the post office is making sure the stupidest person in the class gets it, and the others have to suffer.

My instructor was a rather grouchy but nice older man, who was about as politically correct as well, as an old man usually is, which is none. Though knowledgeable, he often did and said things that pretty much surprised me, as we were in a classroom setting, and I found it pretty unprofessional. But in the end, he was generous when it was time for breaks, and he did his best to make a ridiculous class fun, so I'm not going to go into details here as to what he said and did, as I'm not trying to get the man in trouble if word got out. But someone should tell these people that what they say and do can be repeated, and a lot of the people I met over my time as a CCA sure opened themselves up to a world of grief if I was a sadistic person and wanted to share absolutely everything. But I'm not here to either trash the USPS, or get a hard-working employee into trouble—which is very lucky for them. I'm just here to share my experience as I went through the process.

You'll get your schedule when and where to show up for your LLV training. My training was right across the street from where postal employees park in Boston.

The trucks themselves are simple to use. There are only two things a new driver needs to be aware of. The first is that the driver's seat is on the right side, like a vehicle made in London. This is so when letter carriers deliver mail to curbside mailboxes— like on a long, long road—they can do it from the vehicle, without having to get out. The second is there is no rear window, so if you've ever driven an SUV and had so much junk in the back, say on moving day, that you couldn't use the rearview mirror, and had to back up by using only your side mirrors, then you'll do fine with these little trucks.

The trainers were nice, and totally seemed to get it that the idea of people driving around in circles all day is pretty silly, but still, it's a necessity.

Drive around for six hours in a vehicle, even if it's only in circles, and soon you will feel very comfortable driving said vehicle.

Well, to a point, and I will elaborate later.

The obstacle course wasn't difficult, and as I hold a CDL, these little box trucks were a snap. Comfortable in only using my side mirrors, I whipped around the course, and usually had to slow down or risk crowding the two other CCAs I was training with. Some people in the past trained all alone, just themselves driving around the course in circles, but these days, with the push to hire new carriers, I would be very surprised if you were alone.

Now, I'll admit here, that I was still a little nervous in driving them at the start, simply because the driver's seat is on the right side. I've driven on the left side of the road overseas, and though strange and dangerous at the beginning, as your motor reflexes want you to turn one way, but you need to follow entirely differ-ent rules, it didn't take long before I got the hang of it and almost never made a mistake. (I say almost never because once in a while old habits surface and you have to catch yourself.)

First, with the trainer leading myself and two others, we walked the course. Orange cones were all set up, some in shapes of driveways, others like an intersection, and one in the shape of a snake so that we could pull in and around and then back out.

A few were near the far corner, where there was what could be called a curb, though was just the edge of the lot. Here, fake mailboxes on posts were set up so that we could become familiar with pulling up to a box and sliding mail in without leaving the vehicle. Other times we were instructed to park and leave the truck, then pretend we'd been gone for an hour while delivering, and were asked to quickly give the vehicle a once-over to make sure it was okay: no new dents, or scratches.

But the most important thing you need to remember when you're training with the LLV is to do a few tasks one at a time before you leave the vehicle each time.

You want to curb it, park it, brake it, and take it (the keys).

Here's the deal, no sugar-coating. These trucks are pieces of shit, yes that's right. No instructor or anyone else will tell you this, but they will use any other words they can come up with. Old, tired, well-used, at the end of their life, whatever.

Frankly, these vehicle get the shit beat out of them on a daily basis, and they were never built to last this long. So if you want a blast from the past, hop into one of these 1985 babies and have fun driving around in the snow. Made out of aluminum, they're as light as a feather, and if you're lucky the defrost will work.

These issues hark back to the job freeze, I believe. Any company that uses vehicles on a daily basis, knows that without those vehicles they have no company. But here it is, 2016, and the post office is still using the same vehicles from 1985.

Why? Because the higher-ups didn't want to spend profit on vehicles.

Let the carriers deal with it, no doubt, which seems to be a popular idea at USPS. I'll get into that more later as well.

After we walked the course, the trainer quickly went through the LLV, pointing out this and that. If you can drive a car, and you should, as you needed a valid drivers license to even get this far as a CCA, then nothing in the truck will be a surprise—other than the driver's seat being on the right side, that is.

Then off you go.

You simply begin the course and keep driving around and around and around it for the next two hours.

I want to point out that the three LLVs used for training have excellent heat, and I would have been surprised if they didn't. The trainers would ensure that when they're inside those trucks, they aren't going to freeze to death like a letter carrier would on their route. So the LLVs you use to train in will be in a lot better condition than the others you'll use when out on the street.

For myself, it took minutes to get used to driving on the right side, and fifteen minutes later, I was pretty comfortable driving the thing. It was kind of fun at the beginning, as it's like driving a toy, and is far different than driving a car or SUV.

But within the first hour I was already bored and it quickly became monotonous.

Still, this training is for good reason. You're going to be driving these LLVs everyday, and you need to be comfortable in them. And every time you stop and get out, you need to do what?

Curb it, park it, brake it, and take it (the keys).

When you're on the street delivering, you're quickly going to see how busy you are, and to take the time to put on your seatbelt, or when leaving the LLV, to put on the emergency brake, or even to turn off the engine, will seem like a waste of time and you're not going to bother.

Well, if you choose to do this, you have no one to blame when either the truck gets stolen or it rolls away on its own.

See, the transmissions on the LLVs are crap, which goes back to the whole piece-of-shit idea because they're far too old to still be going. So if you're on a hill, and though you put the vehicle into park, you might get out and begin your route and glance to the side and see your postal vehicle driving by.

Feel free to wave to it, as you're waving goodbye to your job at the same time.

Stealing is one way to get your butt canned immediately, and maybe even jail time, and the other way to guarantee you're getting fired is to let your LLV go for a drive without you in the driver's seat.

Not to mention how embarrassing it must be to go back to the station and explain what happened to the other letter carriers!

I was told by an instructor when I asked, that if you do even one step in the mantra—just one!—there's almost zero chance of a runaway/rollaway happening to you. So if you do them all it simply won't happen—ever.

See, *curb it* means to turn your wheels into the curb, so that if the vehicle began to roll either forwards or backwards, the turned tires will make the LLV swing and hit the curb, thus stopping it from going any further than a few feet.

And the rest is simple and should actually be common practice in the personal vehicles you drive.

As for taking the keys with you each time you leave the LLV, there's an easy solution to that as well.

When you go out on a route, you're going to sign out for an *Arrow* key. This little key will open all the apartment boxes on the route you're delivering to that day and are usually universal for each city. (And don't forget to return it at the end of the day; don't bring it home with you!) To make sure it's not lost, it's required you attach it to the belt loop on your pants. So attach the LLV keys to the arrow key as well, and each time you leave the vehicle you have no choice but to turn off the engine, or else you'll find yourself still attached to the vehicle! But don't worry about being attached. In an emergency, either the belt loop or chain would break if you had to jump out of the seat quickly.

The arrow key is on a very long chain so it will allow you to do this—but more on that later.

*　*　*

Okay, so now five hours have passed and you've driven around the course so many times you could close your eyes and still do it successfully. You know where every cone is and every turn you need to take to get through the course.

But don't get cocky, for though you're comfortable driving the LLV inside the course, when you take your driving test on the street at the end of the day, the situation changes drastically.

Heed my next words, because it's simple to mess up. I had a close call I will explain in a moment, and it was sheer luck I passed the test. Not because I was cocky, or careless, but simple inexperience judging clearances, which can happen to anyone, but hopefully, if you're reading this, there will be zero chance of it happening to you.

The test you take when driving through South Boston, if that is where you're taking it, like I did, is not set up for you to fail.

Far from it.

The instructor just wants to make sure you can drive the LLV without running over old ladies.

One thing I disliked, and I said this to the instructor when we headed out on our test at the end of the day, is that it would have been nice if we could have driven around in the 'real word' for even fifteen minutes before the test began. Here, I could have been taught little things I would need to know, such as distance of where I'm in proportion to the yellow lines on a two-way street.

The moment I pulled out of the lot and onto a main street, I began to drift slightly so that the left side of the vehicle was riding the double yellow line. Now heed this advice 'cause it's good advice. I told the two CCAs who went after me this issue and they were easily able to correct for it when they began to do it too. But being first, I had no one to warn me.

Remember, you're driving on the right side of the vehicle, so as you roll down the street, you have a normal tendency to want to keep some distance from the cars on your right, just like you would in a left-side driving car.

So due to this little lapse, I ended up pushing the left side onto the yellow line.

What you need to keep remembering until it becomes motor reflex, is that you're right there on the edge on the right side, so you need to move the LLV over to the right, so you're two feet or so from parked vehicles.

Then your LLV is inside the lines as you drive down the street.

Now, when I got into my LLV for my test, lucky me, my vehicle was very, and I mean *very* low, on gas. So we had to go to the gas station to fill the tank.

This was almost my undoing I believe.

On the way there, I went as slow as Grandma going to church on Sunday. I made sure to always use signal lights, and I even kept my hands at ten and two to cover my bases.

Other than getting too close to the yellow line while driving down the street, I was doing okay.

But now we pull into the gas station. I've never been in this vehicle in a situation like this, so I take it slow—and I mean real slow.

I pull in, doing my best to line up the vehicle like we all would.

So when I stop the LLV and put it in park and secure it, I was surprised when the instructor points to the metal poles that protect the pumps from errant drivers.

The left side of the vehicle is literally four inches from the metal pole.

He said, "A little close there, aren't you?"

I was shocked, and in a heartbeat realized that I'd had no idea that pole was there and it was simply dumb luck that I'd missed it by a few inches.

Now, I might be wrong on this. For all I knew, because I was going slow, and though close, still unconsciously was doing my best to line up the vehicle, I may have missed the pole more on skill than luck.

But if I am being totally honest here, and why the hell not? Then I was the luckiest bastard in the world, for only four inches had decided if I'd passed or not, as I'm sure hitting a pole while getting gas is a failure.

If you fail the driving test, you have to wait six months before you can reapply for CCA again, and that means going through the entire process from step one anew.

The instructor was waiting for my reply, so you know what I did?

Yup, you betcha.

I lied through my teeth and acted as if I'd planned to get that close.

I said, "Too close? Sure, but a miss is a miss, right? I just wanted to get the truck close for you to pump the gas."

He considered this and I'd like to think didn't see through my probably very bad poker face. Then he added, "Well I guess so, but next time let's not get *that* close, okay?"

I agreed and he hopped out to get gas. While he was pumping the fuel, I studied the pole in the fender mirror and I realized it was probably three inches not four.

Wow, I was so lucky. I figured I needed to play the lottery that night.

When he was finished refueling the LLV and back in the vehicle, I slowly edged out, coming to within two inches of the pole, but still…there's a saying with old time bus drivers. An inch or a foot, a miss is a miss.

The rest of the test was uneventful and when we returned to the lot, I assumed I had passed.

But later I found out that you don't find out whether you passed or not right there. I had taken the test on a Saturday, and I had to return to Orientation on Monday. I discovered later that if you fail the driving test, someone would come into class and tap you on the shoulder and tell you you're done. I found this out at eleven in the morning so if I hadn't been asked to leave then I'd passed.

Lucky me.

Still, kind of a shitty way to do this.

Make someone drive an hour to get to class for a seven AM start time, only for them to tell you that you'd failed the driving test and have to reapply in six months, so go home, you're finished.

So when you leave that day of LLV training, I hope you pass, but there's no guarantee until later, whether you learn if you passed or failed.

Chapter 7
First Day On The Job

The first day I arrived in the Chelsea IMC was pretty overwhelming. Not knowing where to go, or what to do, you could only be led around like a dog on a leash; told to sit here, sign this, do this, ect.

The station itself was a hum of activity, but controlled chaos was a better description.

In many ways, the entire process of the mail arriving, getting scanned and then going out with carriers is almost on autopilot.

Now, in all the stations, there's a manager. Normally, this is someone you shouldn't be seeing unless you're about to get fired or close to it. You shouldn't be working with managers on a daily basis—never.

That's what all the supervisors are for. See, for every ten letter carriers, one supervisor is needed. This can make things rather top-heavy, when it comes to people in charge.

There was a quick talk on safety, which is a massive subject with the post office, and it should be. When a carrier gets hurt, he can't work, which means a valuable employee is off the schedule, which means everyone else has to pick up the slack on an already overloaded system.

Sure, if you happen to slip and fall and are out for a week or so while you heal, it might not seem so bad, but not all injuries are that simple. You could slip and go face-first into stone steps, shattering teeth and maybe even breaking your jaw. You could fall on ice and crack your head open—literally. You could hurt your back so you can barely walk.

Though people make jokes of getting hurt and getting some paid time off, the truth is it's a hell of a risk that your injury won't be long-lasting, so safety is good for everyone.

Now, that's the theory, but in reality, what I saw was of course very different. Whether the place was simply too busy, with not enough people to monitor safety, or there were a lot of incompetent people there, I have no idea.

I only saw what I saw as I walked around.

But before we go any further, I have to introduce the manager of the station, a pompous, overweight man who enjoyed listening to himself talk—someone I felt an immediate lack of respect for and a dislike so strong I would walk to the far end of the large building if it meant avoiding him.

I had a total of three or four exchanges with him, and each one made me dislike the man a little more.

Let me elaborate and you can judge for yourself.

I would like to note that as you get older, you realize the idea that you must dislike your boss is a silly one. People are people. Some are leaders, and some are not. Yes, usually, people who can't do a job move up to management, but even when this happens, if they're decent people with confidence, they can still inspire respect from their employees.

In theory perhaps, but in reality things go a whole lot like what happened to me.

So though myself and another CCA should have been sent right out to be with carrier trainers, so we could begin learning how to set up a route and then go out for the day with said trainer, instead, we were ushered into the manager's office.

The second I entered this man's office, I had an idea who he was, without seeing or hearing him for the first time. I saw that the man had an inferiority complex, even if he didn't know it for himself. The entire office screamed this to me.

The office was as follows.

An over-sized desk in the center, at least twice the size of a normal one you would see in an office setting. To me, the desk was there to intimidate anyone sitting in one of the two chairs facing it. Hell, even the President of the United States, in the Oval Office, doesn't have a desk this size. On the walls were numerous awards, most of which I had no idea what they meant. And the best one of all, a framed newspaper clipping, roughly twenty-plus-years old, of a photo of the manager back when he was a letter carrier. I found this odd as well. Was this there so that I can somehow think to myself, "Hey, this guy is just like me." Huh, that was so far from the truth the moment I saw the man.

Weighing in at around three hundred pounds—all of it in the belly area—the life of being off the streets had been good to him. If this man had to carry mail for even an hour, he would end up huffing and puffing and probably have a coronary right there on someone's steps. Like I said: those that can't teach, manage.

Still, none of this really bothered me too much. After all, managers aren't involved in day to day operations with letter carriers. That's what the supervisors are for. I would only end up seeing this guy in passing now and then while I worked in the station before leaving to do a route.

As I previously said, but want to reiterate one more time; if this guy had an inferiority complex and needed to make himself look important with a large desk, good for him. Why should I care?

But then came the speech. Well, not so much a speech, as the man enjoyed pontificating (this means he likes to hear himself talk, basically) but more of a story he liked to tell new hires.

Now this is something I found very odd, and I shared this with the other CCA I was in the room with later.

As myself and the other man sat in the chairs before the manager, the other CCA to my left, the manager never once made eye contact with me, but as he droned on about how wonderful he was, and what he'd done, he basically was in a two-way conversation with the other CCA.

When I realized this, I began to watch him, wanting to make sure I wasn't imagining it. Yes, it was true. No matter how many times I tried to meet his gaze, he only looked at the other CCA.

But then the manager asked the other CCA what he'd done as a profession before arriving at the station as a new CCA. The other CCA quickly explained how he'd lost his job when working at a family business—not his family however—when a college graduate son retuned home and needed a job. Well, not being family, out he went.

As I listened, I assumed I would be asked next, as wouldn't you expect him to do that? Think about it, you're being introduced to the manager, he wants to meet you, welcome you, he asks the other person you're with what they did before arriving, surely you would think you would be next, that the manager would ask you the very same question.

Well, if you did expect this, you'd have been very, very wrong and would probably feel like I did, which was a little ignored and a few other feelings not worth getting into right now.

No, it's not that I couldn't wait to tell this pompous man what I did before arriving, and in fact, I'd been going through it in my mind to keep it as brief as possible, and though I would have preferred not to have to do it at all, I would also have preferred that decision be mine.

So when the CCA to my left finished his story, and I assumed the manager was going to look at me and ask me the same question, instead he changes the subject and calls in some trainer letter carriers to get us on our way.

What the fuck just happened?

"Am I invisible?" I wondered, about as insulted as someone could get.

But given this manager was a fool in my eyes, and I already disliked him, I certainly wasn't going to brood on it, as I accepted instantly that I was going to have a boss I didn't like nor respected.

I quickly reasoned that this guy simply liked to talk, to hear himself stroking his own ego.

I soon found out from other letter carries that this was exactly the truth, and that everyone I talked to most definitely did not respect the manager. So it appeared my instinct for the guy wasn't unfounded. Many people would be working that morning, setting up their routes, while saying what a screw-up the guy was.

And it's never a good thing to arrive at a new job and everyone thinks the manager is an idiot.

I want to add here that due to the long speech the manager gave to myself and the other CCA, and though I was able to go out later that day with a letter carrier to train me, the other CCA I was with ended up getting stuck inside the building for the entire day because his trainer had to leave and get out on the street, not able to wait any longer for the manager to release us.

So that CCA got zero training that day for what he was hired for, simply so the manager could pontificate to a couple of newbies who had no choice but to sit and listen. That CCA ended up simply moving packages around the station, and though he was working, in the end he was hired to be a letter carrier, and the sooner he got his training, the sooner he could get out there on his own, so by him not training, every letter carrier suffers down the road when an extra body is needed on a route.

There is one more important thing I was told by this manager when forced to listen to him, as myself and the other CCA were basically a captive audience. I mean, it's not like I could have excused myself because I didn't want to hear this guy bragging about himself. I was as trapped as a human being could be and under control of another person—something I did not like one bit, especially as for many years I was self-employed. But then, no one likes to be turned into someone else's bitch, to be blunt about it.

When the manager went into his talk about safety he said something that rather shocked me. It went like this:

If you slip and fall or something serious like that, we as employees need to notify someone when we return so it can be documented, but if you're out there and you accidentally whack your hand or maybe bend a figure the wrong way, don't bother filing anything. He then explained that something small was an annoyance to file, and when we the employee file an accident notice, there's so much paperwork to do, all because you whacked your hand on a railing. So don't bother to do it unless it's something serious.

Now, like I said, I knew a lot more than a lot of people in how USPS works before even taking the job, and even the CCA to my left would have known that didn't make sense, as the man was competent and intelligent. I don't know what went through his mind but I know what went through mine. "Shit, is this guy fucking serious! This manager is a weasel of the highest caliber."

See, if you so much as get a splinter while on the job, and you're a smart person, get it documented. If you fall and don't report it, and three days later wake up with back pain, how the hell are you going to prove you're in pain because of an on-the-job fall? Simple, you can't, and obviously this manager wants to keep his safety record down, even if it means denying you when you're hurt because you were too stupid to report the incident. So no matter what kind of accident, no matter how small; if you get hurt, fill out a report on it, because that weasel and others just like him will be doing their best to deny you your claim.

Chapter 8
Forget Everything You Learned In Orientation

That's right. Forget everything you were just taught before arriving at your assigned station, because if you don't, you're going to go crazy.

See, what they talked about in those classes was what USPS is supposed to be on paper, what people in rooms in fancy buildings with far too large a salary for what they do have set down as doctrine.

But now you're going to be on the streets, actually doing the job, and unfortunately, almost everything you learned is not feasible in a real-time function. For one thing, if you spent as much time in the station doing all the paperwork you were taught, you would never leave to actually deliver the mail.

So forget it all, simply put it out of your mind, for everything you need to know will be taught to you when and if it's needed.

So to continue my first day, I was finally ushered out of the manager's office and handed off to my trainer for the day; it was time to actually learn the art of being a mail carrier first-hand.

My OJT (On the Job Trainer) was a man named Tim, who had been in the post office for over twenty years. One thing I can say about Tim is that the man knows his job well, and the post office is getting value for every dime they pay him. He was like a robot the entire day.

He never stopped to take a break, nor eat, and if I hadn't asked to use the bathroom later in the day, and he also took advantage of the facilities, I would have begun wondering if the post office had built robots and that was who I was with all day.

To repeat myself yet again: it's the long-time postal carriers and the CCAs that had been there for at least six months or more, that are ensuring the viability of the post office.

These *regular* carriers, which means they're full time with benefits, are the only reason in my opinion the post office is still a functioning entity. If they ever lose these full time carriers, such as they all quit and go somewhere else, overnight the postal system will collapse.

Don't believe me? Well, by the time this book is finished, I think you'll see my point.

In many ways the letter carrier is autonomous to the rest of the postal system. When you deliver a route, there are ten to eleven 'scans' that need to be scanned with the tracking gun. These scans are a way to keep track of the letter carrier, to see where he is and how fast he's delivering on any given day.

Now, in the old days of delivering mail, say before the coming of the internet, being a mailman was a very different job.

A few examples are as follows.

One letter carrier I knew of, where I live outside of Boston, would 'run' the route, which means he would either literally run or would walk much faster than was required. He would also skip his lunch to take later, at the end of the day. Then, he would finish early and with over an hour or more of free time, would drive over to the beach and get some sun on the company's dime.

Another example was of a retired letter carrier. This man worked in Boston, and he would finish early, park his truck on Washington St, and catch a movie while still on the clock.

Of course, nowadays, with global positioning (GPS) in the scanners or even in the vehicles, those days are long gone.

But one thing I quickly figured out at the Chelsea station is that they are so overwhelmed, no one is checking scans anyway, so even if you missed some, it would be a while before anyone questioned you. Still, if you're out there, just do the job they hired you to do and you won't get into any trouble.

Once you're out on the road and away from the office, the job is very different. Now you're basically working alone and need to be responsible enough to do the job, without anyone looking over your shoulder. The only way anyone at the office would know you're doing a bad job is if a postal customer complained, and though that will happen no matter how good you think you're doing, if you do the rest well and follow the rules laid down, it won't happen often. And even if it does, you should have a reason why you did this or that, or missed a scan.

But I'm getting ahead of myself. First, we need to do all the responsibilities in the office, long before we head out to deliver the mail.

Now, the main thing a carrier does each morning is 'throw' the mail. This is something that though it's now 2016, hasn't changed at all since the first days of the postal system when actual routes were created.

Think of a small cubicle about seven feet tall and three feet wide with a small desk or ledge on each side to place the mail. On each side are rows, usually five or so high. Street names and address are on these rows. The streets are set up by 'hits,' which is a simple term for when a carrier parks their LLV, gets out, and does a loop of the street. They start in one place, go down the street, cross over to the other side, then follow it to a certain point, then cross over again and finish by the LLV. Then they drive to another spot close by, usually the next street, and do it again. This way there isn't much wasted walking time. Simple right? The concept certainly sounds simple.

Sure, in theory, but once more, when we're through with this book and you stuck it out with me, you're going to see how far from the truth that really is.

Machines now sort most of the mail, and they arrive each morning in long tubs, but despite this, only a real human being can do it all correctly. The machines constantly make mistakes, and those are called *miss-sorts*. Each day you'll get a stack of mail that was on other routes but was for your route. So you begin each morning with sorting mail, or 'throwing' it, on your route, placing it in the slots for each address the mail is assigned to.

Sound hard?

No, of course not. It's very simple.

This is a lot like playing solitaire. If you played the same game long enough, and the cards never shifted, but remained in place, you would quickly become adept at the game. So as long as you do a route more than once and it becomes repetitive, you'll find throwing on that route is easy.

But, and keep this in mind. As a CCA, your job is to fill in anywhere a letter carrier is needed. Maybe someone called in sick, or got hurt, or took vacation time. So what that means is if you're placed in a large station like I was, with five or six cities, you will probably be on a new route each day. Basically, it means each day you come to work will be your first day working there.

Sure, you'll know what to do in general, but if you don't know where to put the mail in the rows, it's going to take a lot longer than if you'd done it before.

This matters because you'll have supervisors giving you grief for taking too long when at the end of the day you have to call them to say you have hours to go and they want you back, as its getting dark.

See, that wonderful manager I told you about? Well, he instituted a policy that every letter carrier had to be back by six PM. So if you have a thirty minute drive time from your route, you need to finish by 5:30. Add all the packages now that need to be delivered daily, and the fact you don't know the route, and that you left the office late because you don't know the route, and you're never finishing in time. So when you call in to say you need help, be prepared to listen to them complaining.

Other offices don't do this. Though in theory they would want their letter carrier back by six as it's dark out there in the winter, it's not a mandatory rule, so you don't have to either take crap from management or basically be running around like an idiot to finish on time. It's also important to note that while these carriers are basically rushing, if they got hurt, it would be on them, because USPS says over and over that safety comes first. But lucky me, I was assigned to Chelsea and once more I realized a short commute isn't always a good thing, and that an organized station with good management is much more important.

So the saying of 'caught between a rock and hard place' is never as fitting as when working as a letter carrier.

Okay, let's start at the beginning of the day, so you can get an idea how it would go.

You start at seven or seven-thirty in the morning, go to your route, where the little cubicle is, and throw the mail. Then you take any items that are considered *flats*, which is a simple term for magazines, catalogs and the like. Those you 'throw' as well. Then, when it's all done, you take each 'hit' down in the order it will be delivered. Remember what hit means? It's simply the armful of mail for each section on the route.

When all that's done, you get to sort your packages for the day.

Now, I'm going to set aside an entire chapter dedicated to Amazon packages, but for now I'm just going to say that most of what you'll be delivering as far as parcels go will be from Amazon.

Depending on the city, you may have more or less than other routes. Some routes get one large bin, others can get three and four bins.

What's funny is the packages are so abundant now that there are enough to keep each letter carrier busy for an eight hour shift, but on top of that, you still have to deliver letter mail, magazines and pick up mail if it's left out for you.

So to reiterate: USPS now moves enough parcels each day to support having all their full-time employees, but those same employees have to deal with packages AND still do all the duties that have kept the post office afloat for years. So you're basically doing two jobs for the price of one.

Not too bad if you're on USPS' side, I might say.

Sucks pretty bad if you're a letter carrier though.

Chapter 9
It's Only Hard If You've Never Done It Before

Watching my trainer go through the motions of setting up the route for the day was impressive.

Though I knew he'd done the route for years and probably could have been throwing mail with his eyes closed, it was still fascinating to watch. Of course, when he let me throw some I was woefully pitiful. Not knowing the streets and numbers of the houses, it took me forever.

Like I said before, this part is just a memory game, and anyone tossed into this blindly would have been in the same situation, but it still felt incredibly frustrating to want to move faster and not be able to. (This was one of the reasons I quit; the first one being I simply didn't want to work for that pompous manager. Each reason I quit by itself wouldn't have made me leave, but when I total up all the reasons later, then you can decide if you would have stayed in my position.)

What? You didn't think I was actually still there, did you? Did you think I was working sixty-plus hours a week and wrote this book on the side?

Not bloody likely.

So, to get back to me throwing mail in a very pitiful way.

It was painfully obvious it would take days on a single route to get to a point that I could actually make some progress, and be a productive worker, but what I was quickly told (and I filed away to consider if I wanted to keep the job) was that I would probably be on a different route each and every day.

So each day would be like the first day on the job.

I think anyone can agree that when you begin a job it's hard. You don't know what's going on next, when you can take a break, when the rush comes or if there is one. You need to play it by ear, to kind of roll with it for the first few days, so you can get a feel for how the job flows.

Usually, by the beginning of the second week, the job comes easier to you, whatever it might be. Now you know your schedule, can look at the clock and plan for what comes next.

All these things are what make a job tolerable, the fact that you're comfortable in your environment.

But what if your environment keeps changing—every single day. Whether it's because you're in a new city, it's raining, snowing, or all of the above, so that each day will be like it's your first, and all the indecisiveness that will come with it.

Of course, within USPS and if it was a perfect world, why couldn't they see if there was a route open, say on absolutely no one wants, and assign that one to you when you arrive. After even a week you would be pretty comfortable, and you know what? Your productivity would triple because you knew where you were going each day.

Well, in a perfect world lots of things would be better.

But this is reality, so at USPS, they'll put you where you're needed. Someone is on vacation, sick, whatever, you're there. So if there are literally hundreds of routes scattered across five cities, some of them major cities around Boston or wherever you might be posted, you're in for one hell of a ride.

But back to my first day of training.

My trainer showed me three large containers (bins) filled with packages, ninety-five percent of them all from Amazon. (Now to put this in perspective, on the next Sunday I worked only delivering packages, on that day there were only two bins, and there were about ninety parcels that were delivered and took about four hours.)

These three bins of parcels would be delivered today along with all the mail, magazines and good old junk mail we all get everyday. The post office calls junk mail 'Bulk Mail' however, but it is what it is. Call a horse a duck and it doesn't make it a duck. Still, bulk mail is the post office's bread and butter, or at least it was before Amazon. Bulk mail is one of the reasons USPS is still successful, despite the decline of letter mail due to the creation of emails. So before you even step out of the door to head to your LLV, you might be feeling overwhelmed. Try to work through it. There's a saying in USPS. It'll get lighter before it gets heavier.

That's because when you're delivering a 'hit,' as you go to each home or building, you're taking mail from your bundles, and before you know it, you're on the last house and your arms are empty. Well, at least until you begin the next hit. Still, the truck gets emptier as the day goes on.

Okay, back to my first day. Tim and myself wheel the bins—which are about waist height and are roughly five feet wide—full of parcels and mail, out to the vehicle we're using for the day. Because I need a seat, too, and LLVs only have a driver's seat, we get a leased minivan to use for the day.

Tim quickly begins putting parcels at the front of the van, sorting them as he knows he will need to deliver them. Now, if I was alone, I would have been clueless and I can't see how I would have been able to do what he was doing in any sense of a timely manner.

But hell, it was my first day. Today my job was to watch and learn, not set up a route on my own.

Once all the packages were in the van, the letters and magazines were added, and once more in the order Tim knew they would go.

Once all the mail was loaded, there was one more vital task to attend to, and I can't say how truly important it will be to you.

Use the bathroom, because unless you wear Depends' diapers, you might find yourself in a difficult situation later.

That was something else I wasn't looking forward to having to deal with. People in any job where a bathroom is located nearby, such as working in an office building or any building for that matter, have no idea what it's like for people with jobs where bathrooms aren't easily accessible. Policeman, construction workers who are on a single street for the day, and of course letter carriers, all have to juggle their jobs while keeping in mind their body has needs that will not be ignored. Of course, you can train your body a lot, but still there's a ritual we all follow if you eat and drink on a regular basis.

Now, if you're on a route you've done before, you're going to learn where to go and at what time. But what if you're on a different route every single day, and are delivering in places you have no idea where you are?

That's why, oh every once in a while, there's a story on the news about a male postal carrier peeing in someone's bushes. Terrible? Sure, if you don't understand the reasons behind the guy's actions, which were that the poor guy had to go. What was he supposed to do? Wear a diaper?

Just another layer of the hardships of the job, so be ready for it in however you plan on dealing with it, and hope like hell you don't have a day where you need to be on the toilet every fifteen minutes.

Come to think of it, you might as well call in sick that day.

But back to my first day.

So the bathroom situation is addressed, with a few more tiny matters to attend to before setting out for the day. One is get a scanner, so you can do all those Amazon scans that are mandatory. From what I gathered, pretty much any other scan you do all day can be overlooked if you don't do it, but make damn sure Amazon packages get scanned. In many ways, and I've said it before, you work for Amazon, only your paycheck still says USPS on it. A technicality that will be addressed in the future no doubt.

Now, just before you head out, you're supposed to check the *hot case*, which is where miss-sorted mail is resorted. You want to make sure there's no First class mail there that was added after the first time you went there. See, in the morning, you swing by this case and grab mail for your route to throw it, then hours later before you leave, you re-check.

One carrier I trained with did this, but the second one on a different day didn't bother, not feeling the need. This is where your own sense of workmanship will come into play. See, when you check one last time, you *scan* the hot case with its bar code with your scanner, to prove you'd been there one last time, but other than the scan, no one will ever know if you actually bothered to take the mail if there was more.

I saw this a lot. Other than the scans, whether the actual job was getting done was up in the air. The almighty scans seemed to be the way the people making the big bucks figured they could control their workers, but in reality it was a really silly method. But most people do their job correctly and take pride so none of it really matters anyway.

Once more the mail moves simply because the people at the bottom, namely the letter carriers, move it and know what they're doing. Get a carrier who either doesn't care or is lazy, and you the postal customer are pretty much screwed.

Okay, so once you scanned the hot case, you then scan one more barcode, which is around the exit door where you leave the building. This scan tells people who are watching from on high that you're finally leaving the *office* and are going *out on the street*.

You also use you timecard to change from office time to street time. All this is simply because they want to know how long you were in the building, and how long you were out on the street delivering mail. When you return at the end of the day, you use your time card again to enter that you're now back in the office, as well as scan that barcode on the door with your scanner to document it as well.

Lots of scans. So if you don't understand it all, don't worry, once you do it once or twice, trust me, it isn't hard at all.

But don't worry, for soon I am sure, if they have their way, USPS is just going to implant you when you're hired so they can keep track of you all the time that way. Joking now, but you just wait and see.

Okay, all the scans are done, you've made sure to have your Arrow key on you to open all those mail boxes in multi-family homes, you've changed your time card from *office* to *street* time, so there's nothing else to do but hop in your LLV or minivan and it's off to deliver the mail.

Now the fun really starts.

Chapter 10
The Mail Box Is Where?

Before I start this chapter, I want to point something out. In the post office, accountability is almost zero.

If a clerk throws a package onto the wrong route, no one will talk to them about it later. If mail gets miss-delivered, no one has to explain why. If a package is delivered to the wrong address, and the addressee says they never got it, and it can be proved they never got it, no carrier will *ever* have to explain themselves.

In all my years working for companies, restaurants, ect, I've never seen a job with an accountability level so low. It seems that no matter what someone does, with the exception of stealing, they will almost never answer for their actions. In the end, it all comes down to the personal work ethic of each individual, and with morale pretty low, shit, we're all in trouble if we like to get our mail.

All right, back to my first day on the job. But to quickly recap the first day in all its detail would be tedious, for all I did was follow Tim, my carrier trainer, around on his route while he delivered. Other than shadow him from house to house, there really wasn't much else to do. Though I asked the poor guy a million questions so I could learn as much as possible.

It was on the second day, when I was given 'hits' to deliver myself, that I really got a taste what I was in for when out there alone.

Luckily it was a nice day out, as far as no gusts of wind or rain or snow. It was around twenty-five degrees out however, but if you dress warm, you'll find the cold isn't too much of a bother. I know right? You'd think I must be lying, if you're not someone who works outside. I didn't believe it myself until being out there.

Wear long johns, and three layers of shirts and sweaters, and along with a warm jacket and hat, you're actually quite warm. And when you begin walking, carrying mail, climbing steps, you'll soon find yourself even becoming hot.

Many of the older carriers, who have been there for years, prefer winter to summer, as at least in the winter they can remove layers as they get warm. In the summer, when it's ninety degrees and humid, there's nothing you can do but remain hot and sweaty.

The main thing I found utterly ridiculous as a letter carrier were the locations of mailboxes and house numbers. Now, if you've never had a reason to do this—and why would you?— there's zero uniformity when it comes to placements of mailboxes, or receptacles.

If you remember the *Tonight Show* with Johnny Carson, where he would place a sealed letter to his head and then ask a question, then open the letter for the punch line, this is what it's like delivering on a route you've never been on before.

As you approach a house or multi-apartment home, your eyes are going to start roving. If you're like me, the first place you look is to the left or right of the front door, as to me, that would be the best place to put a mailbox. But don't assume this, for some people must be high on drugs or drunk when they decided to place their mailbox. Some were hidden, so you would have to climb the ten stairs to take you to the front porch, then when on the landing before the front door, you would then have to turn around and look down around knee-height, to see the boxes attached to the railing. Other times the mailbox is nowhere to be found on the front of the house, because the owner wants the mail delivered to a side door.

Now this is worth a chapter in its own right, but I won't bother. But some people are so self-absorbed, they assume if *they* know where they want their mail, then *you* should, too. If you're lucky, there might be a small, three-inch, handwritten note on the front door, telling you where to deliver their mail, the ink usually faded from years of weather exposure.

Frankly, I got tired of playing the mailbox game pretty quickly and I would simply toss the mail between the front screen door. If they didn't like it, I really wasn't worried about it.

Now, if you think I had a bad attitude by doing this, just let me see how long you take doing this. I'm not talking about delivering on a route you know, and have done before, I'm talking about being on a new route each day, where you have no idea where anything is.

But we're not done yet when it comes to where people want their mail, oh hell no.

Some people want you to walk down a driveway to a side door, like I said before, but others want their mail in a box on a garage at the end of a really long driveway—you should do the walking, not them, is their reasoning. Others want it in the mail slot on their front door, but most of the time the slots are about four inches long. Have you seen the size of most of the mail nowadays? With the exception of standard mail of course. So yup, inside the front screen door it goes. And as for Headliners, I didn't even bother with them. I placed them on the porch and used something heavy to keep them from blowing away, or used an elastic to wrap them up when my hands weren't too full.

That's another thing as well. Maybe you'll do better than I did, but when you have three bundles in your hands, each one five to size inches thick, if not larger, and now you need to juggle it all while trying to shove eight inches of mail into a four inch slot, you tell me what you'd do? I made a joke that it would be nice if I could have a small table on wheels I could pull alongside me, so I could put things down when I needed to.

And be careful for dogs and mail slots in doors. One carrier told me a story how each time they slid the mail in the slot, it would get sucked in like a Hoover vacuum was on the other side. The dog would take it; like it was being fed mail for lunch! So watch those fingers, because you never know what's on the other side of that mail slot.

So where is that damn mailbox, you may ask? Well, forget about that part, what about if you can't even find the house it's attached to?

You think this might sound silly, but I tell you, it's unbelievable out there. Houses are built behind other houses, so that unless you know the home is there, you'll go right by it. Sometimes, there are tiny little streets with three houses on them, and each of those houses are multi-family. I went to one street, a small dead end, and there had to be at least six addresses there. I found most of them but not all.

One reason is the areas I delivered had a lot of immigrants, and these people do not feel the need to put their names on their mailboxes, or worse, they ALL DO!

I mean, I went to some homes in Somerville and Everett where I could have sworn a Third World country resided there. I'm talking five mailboxes on the front of the house, with a total of over twenty different names between them.

I would stand there, sorting mail for each box, trying to figure out where it all went. And almost always, and I mean always, the names are handwritten messily, so I can barely make out Santos, or Menendez, or some name I can't pronounce, let alone write down.

What a goddamn mess!

I learned from another trainer that if I want to be productive in my ninety days and not go over in how long it takes to deliver, to just don't bother trying to sort it all out. Take everything for that multi-family, pick a mailbox, and just shove it all in there and move on.

Besides, half the mail would end up being for people who had moved months ago. See, it seems most of the immigrants on these routes don't put in forwarding addresses when they move, so the mail keeps coming long after they're gone.

If I mentioned this before, I'm going to say it again. At Orientation they will badger you about your first ninety days, how if you screw up you might get canned.

This is so much bullshit it's insane.

Listen, the USPS is so desperate for people that if the Union let them, they'd be going to Home Depot to get workers that are hanging around outside. Unless you steal, let your truck do a rollaway with you in it or not, or call in sick five days in a row repeatedly, they aren't going to fire you; they can't, they need people too much. If you do your best and make a few mistakes, no one is looking to fire you.

But back to where is the mailbox?

Sometimes you need to go inside the house, to a mud room or sun room, or some fucking room that at least gets you out of the cold for a second or two. Here, you may find a mailbox, a slot, or if none of the above, just drop the mail on the floor. One house liked the mail in a small wooden box to the side, with no names on it, nothing. I only knew this because the letter carrier told me.

I asked him: "Now how in God's name would I have known that's where this customer wants their mail if you didn't tell me? I'm not a bloody mind reader?"

He just shrugged, as there was no answer.

So don't be afraid to try doors to see if they're unlocked if no mailbox is in sight. You're on your appointed rounds, a government employee. No one is going to accuse you of breaking and entering when you're on Safari while searching for a mailbox like a fucking archeologist seeking the Holy Grail.

And yes, it will seem like that when you're on a route you've never been on before.

Okay so I'm going to jump ahead to my third day of training, but before I go into what it was like being out there, doing sections of a route I'd never seen before, I need to share another 'douche bag moment' from my manager.

When you're in Orientation, they explain about hazards on your route, such as broken stairs, dangerous dogs, hanging ice or overgrown shrubs that are growing into the walkway so bad that you need to whip out a machete and play Indiana Jones to get to the front door.

In these circumstances you put in a Hazard card that goes on the route in the address slot for that residence, to warn other carriers there's a potential danger, or worse, the mail for the place is on *Hold* until they've corrected the issue.

Now, for someone like me, who's going to be on a different route daily, this shit seemed pretty damn important. How do I know there's a bad step if no one tells me? See, I don't want to trip, go face first into a porch landing, and have to gum my food for the rest of my life or worse, have to suck it through a Silly straw. No job is worth that, and for sixteen bucks an hour, even less.

The second letter carrier I was with had been in for twenty or so years, but unlike Tim, this guy was a little more beaten down by the job. He did his job, but he wasn't going crazy over it in doing more than he needed to. Maybe it was because the route I did with him wasn't actually his own route, he was just doing it while the regular carrier who owned the route was out sick after falling and cracking his head open. I can see why he'd be this way. It's not his route. What's the point of working hard, busting his butt to clean it up, only to have the regular carrier take it back later. All that work for nothing. And like I said, no one's patting you on the back; you're not getting an anything for all that extra work.

In a nutshell, no one gives a shit but you.

So if you own the route, sure, keep it clean and tight, but if you don't, well, that's up to you and your work ethic.

But think of it this way. When each day you come in, do a different route, and have to take Headliners Wednesday thru Saturday, then you come in on a Saturday to find you have ALL the Headliners to do because the other carriers ignored them, and when you try to complain that you're stuck with them all, your supervisors tell you "tough shit" then let's see how much extra you want to do in the future.

Doing the job doesn't mean you're going to get to a point you don't care about it, but you'll find that happy medium on how much TO care.

Okay to get back to that moment I was talking about.

So while I was delivering the previous day, I came to a house where there were three steps and no railings. The second step was made of a solid piece of Indian stone. The entire piece had collapsed from ill-repair and was lying on its side on the first step. So unless I remembered to bring by mountain climbing gear, I wasn't going to get up the steps without hopping or jumping.

But I wasn't an invalid and because it was only three steps, I jumped onto the landing, delivered the mail and left, figuring I would ask the carrier why the hell there wasn't a Hold on that home. I just figured that if it had been snowing, the stairs covered with snow and ice, and I would have tried to climb them, not knowing what waited beneath, I could have fallen hard.

See, that letter carrier seemed to forget there are days he calls in sick or other reasons he might not do the route, and when he wasn't there, someone else, probably new to the job, would have to deliver there. Some of these guys figure they're the only one delivering these routes, but that's not always the case.

I took a photo of the house and stairs and made sure the address number was in the picture. Later, when I was finished with that loop, and I asked the carrier I was with, he simply shrugged and said we deliver to it anyway. He was a man who had been beaten down by the system I already said. He wasn't going to do any more than needed because he knew the people above didn't have his back.

Well, the next morning, day four of my training, I decided that house bugged the shit out of me, and if the carrier wasn't going to do something about it, I would. So I walked over to a supervisor for the city I was in and showed him the picture.

As I raised my phone with the image on the screen to show him, his head snapped back like I was going to punch him. "Wow," I thought, "skittish much."

He then looked at the photo but probably due to the size, didn't understand what he was seeing, so I tried to explain, but either this man wasn't too bright or he really wasn't interested in anything I had to say. I pick the latter. After all, I was this new CCA, nothing I said could have mattered.

So I tried to explain what the image was for and why, and I made sure to add that the step had just fallen, that because it just happened, that was why the carrier on the route every day hadn't put a Hold in. After all, even if the carrier I was with was a lazy bastard, I wasn't looking to get him burned.

Now, I was warned by this other carrier not to bother about the stairs, but in a way, I guess I had to find out for myself how truly fucked up this station was. I needed to know that the carrier wasn't just being lazy, that the upper management wasn't that bad for his city at least. Remember, there were five cities in this station. Some supervisors in charge of carriers in one of the other cities there may have been excellent. I never met them, so can't say. People are people, some are good and some are incompetent. But this book is about my personal experience, seen through my eyes only.

Okay, but before I tell you what happened, I want to share with you how I imagined the scenario would occur, and who would say what, ect.

I would go to the supervisor, show him the picture. If he didn't understand it I would explain what he was seeing. H would simply nod, say thanks for bringing this to his attention, and do one of two things. One, he would make a note of it somewhere, the house and street, to put in a Hold himself, or two: he would make a note of it and ask the regular carrier to do it. There, no drama, and a dangerous house now had a Hold on it so no one would deliver there and get hurt.

Either way I figured what I was doing would be considered a good thing, something to be praised. No, not like I was awesome, but that though I was only days new, I did the right thing.

In most places, and most jobs, I think that's how it would have happened.

But, I made a large mistake.

Commons sense isn't here, this is USPS.

I was warned by people I knew who worked as letter carriers how it was but still, to see it happen for myself was truly amazing, and one of the reasons I'm writing this book.

Like I said, the supervisor didn't seem to comprehend what I was telling him, though I believe I explained myself quite well. After a minute or so, I realized all I'd been told was true and I decided to pretend I never tried.

I said, "Never mind, my mistake," and with a polite wave, turned to go back to the route I was on with the trainer.

But this shit wasn't over, oh no. The manager had walked over and he saw a perfect time to pontificate, to make himself look important.

He stops me from leaving and demands, yes, I'm not exaggerating, he demands I come back and explain what I wanted.

Well, not wanting to argue with the guy, as it would serve no purpose, I returned and he asked to see the photo. I did as he asked and he didn't understand what he was seeing either, and then began a speech on how I needed to be clearer on explaining myself.

Now, when I was younger, I might have argued with him, explaining that I was pretty damn clear, and the supervisor doesn't seem to comprehend basic things, like a Hold on a house, but age grants wisdom. Seeing this guy for what he was, I knew anything said would fall on deaf ears. As a leader, this man was woefully inadequate. All he inspired from me was contempt.

He then began to berate me, right there in the center of all the routes, and frankly, I can't write about what he said because his words were now falling on my deaf ears and I kinda tuned him out. I just stood there and let him go on and on. When he was finished I gave him a "Yes, sir," and seriously, I tasted bile while doing it, but I wasn't going to get fired due to this asshole. We all know assholes are everywhere and we can never let them dictate how we lead our lives, whether personal or professional, only how they affect each of us.

He then finished with, "And now you've wasted eight minuets of my valuable time."

I blinked in surprise at that one. He never should have gotten involved in the first place! Like I mentioned earlier, managers are not seen in stations usually, only supervisors. You should never have day to day dealings with a manager, whether they're a great person or an idiot. They don't do what this guy did, but unfortunately for me, yeah, this guy likes to get in everyone's face.

So I returned to the route cubicle and then had to basically apologize to no end to the carrier I was with, explaining what I did and why, and how I sincerely regretted it. I also promised that manager would *never* speak to me like that again in public. If he tried, I would tell him to stop, then I would ask for my Union rep to be present, which all in all is a massive waste of everyone's time. But I didn't want to lose my temper and get fired for telling the guy to go to hell.

This manager talked to me like I was a no one, like I was beneath him to the point I deserved no respect. I only wish when I'd quit later, that it was his fat ass out there delivering because I wasn't there and the station was short one more body. Of course, that would never happen.

If you're looking for a job where you feel valued, then this one might not be for you. Yes, you will get paid, but I doubt you'll feel any sense of accomplishment as no one will ever tell you "Great job!" But you're here to get paid, not get pats on the back.

The only reason I bother to point out this little altercation, was because it was a slap in the face, a wake up call to all I'd been told by regular carriers but truly couldn't believe unless experiencing it first hand. So, this guy had just berated me for what any quality manager would have considered a good thing, and now, feeling pretty pissed off, I had to go out and deliver mail all day. And you wonder why you hear stories of mailmen tossing mail into dumpsters? This is the reason; for when you feel like your working for people who truly could give a shit about you, then usually, you don't feel like doing a good job.

But despite all the above, keep this tidbit of something positive in mind, as it's what will probably keep you going each day.

Once you're out on the street, and the supervisors and managers are left back at the office, you're basically working alone, doing your route, the responsibility of doing it right on you alone. Even if you didn't do it right, it would be days if not weeks before anyone found out and questioned you. So it's your work ethic and only yours that's in play now, and I liked that part a lot. I had to do a job and no one was standing behind me watching me. And when you return at six at night or later, the managers and supervisors are *long* gone, so you don't have to see them.

Most carriers will tell you they aren't big fans of being in the office in the morning, but once they're out on the street delivering, they enjoy the job.

There was a little bit more fallout due to my trying to get a Hold on that house. I guess the regular carrier was taken aside and kind of yelled at about it. I felt bad but I will be honest here. If the guy had done his job and not been lazy about it, then none of it would have happened to begin with.

I found out later from another carrier of over thirty years that whether you're a CCA, or a regular carrier, there are good ones and bad ones, lazy ones and hardworking ones. You can decide who is what for yourself.

But I will admit, I filed this all away for whether or not I wanted to keep doing the job. I was free to leave at any time, and was really doing the job as I considered it a challenge. Sure, money was nice as well, but I just wanted to see if I could do it, as I knew it was a really tough job. How tough, I had no idea till I tried it for myself.

So I never went in with any conceptions of being able to do the job and actually was pretty sure I wouldn't be able to do it—not if I didn't truly have to.

I wonder what that regular carrier really thought of me after getting talked to in what I'm sure was the manager's same disrespectful tone. The carrier never showed any disdain if that's how he felt, and I actually think that he'd been doing the job long enough that he knew when to let stuff just roll off his back. I'd like to think that me apologizing and admitting profusely that I'd fucked up and *never* should have said anything, that I needed to see how management dealt with issues for myself, or I would never learn how to react when issues arise, made the carrier not be so angry with me.

Once more I want to point out how when you're in the station in the morning, controlled chaos would be an understatement. There is mail everywhere, bins full of packages at each route; you can barely walk around. For someone new, you have no idea who is in charge, where to go for help, completely lost. It's a really terrible feeling to have and know it's not going to get better for quite a while—if ever.

Let me toss something else out there that's relevant to when you're out on your own. When you go out on a new route, one you've never done before, you're supposed to get maps of the area. Yeah, maybe at other stations this is going to happen but not in Chelsea. They expect you to use your cell phone and look up what you need.

But my phone didn't really do that well. It's a small phone, and though it gets emails, using the internet isn't something I make a habit of with it. The screen's too small. So be aware of that one. For me, yet again, I filed this little nugget away under pros and cons, this item being the latter.

Chapter 11
I Don't Know Where I'm Going

On my third day of CCA training, I was with a different trainer than Tim, and as we went through the morning with the new OJT, I set up the route, and did everything I explained in the previous chapter. Of course, I didn't do all of, it, but I did throw most of the route myself, as well as throw Headliners, which will be discussed in the next chapter.

The rest of the setup was done by my trainer, and I was constantly asking questions to make sure I had it all down.

On a side note, I asked both trainers if there could be a time when we could stop for a few minutes, and I could write down each consecutive step I would need to do when on my own. Now, I would think that would be something already done, especially considering how many new CCAs are coming in each month, but that would mean common sense was a factor, and though I was told before I got the job by letter carriers I knew that common sense wasn't a big factor with USPS, I found out for myself they were entirely correct.

There was never a free moment to get this information. We would rush all morning to set up the route and then get it all in the LLV or minivan, then we would rush all day delivering the mail, and then we would rush to return to the office, because we all needed to be finished by six o'clock, and that included travel time from the route. This wasn't feasible, but the manager said it was because he didn't want people delivering in the dark; I have to cry bullshit on that one. He was doing this so he could try and save on the overtime, as during Christmas, overtime was given away freely; it wasn't an issue, only keeping the mail moving, and making sure parcels were delivered on time for Christmas.

I don't know this for a fact, so I will admit that here, but anyone who understands how business works knows overtime is a losing bet for any successful business, and they want to curtail it whenever possible.

So if you're out there delivering mail, and you're new and know you won't be done in time, around three o'clock or so, call in to the office, get a supervisor on the phone, and tell them you need help finishing or you're going to be returning late. They can either authorize your overtime or they will send someone out to help you by taking an hour or more of your hits.

Oh, and the way to answer a supervisor when you're sent out with four hours of work and they want it done in three, is to tell them, "I'll do my best."

Words to live by in USPS. How can you promise something you don't know if you can do or not? And how can you do a task if not given enough time? Well, you're going to find out first-hand because these are what USPS does to their employees every day.

So, "I'll do my best," means just that, as that's all you can do.

But back to that checklist that would have made my job not only easier, but make me more productive.

Wasn't going to happen; there wasn't so much as a few moments to get this. So the next day, when I was on day four of my training, and I knew after only two more days I would be on my own, I had decided that the training I was getting was still not sufficient for the job I was being asked to do. Now, if I didn't give a shit and wasn't worried, then it probably wouldn't have mattered, but when I'm tasked to do a job, well, goddammit, I will do it right or to the best of my abilities given what I know, and If I don't have the tools to do it right, I'm going to speak up.

But in the Chelsea station, my speaking up would have fallen on deaf ears, so realizing it would be hopeless, I once more filed this little gem in the pros and cons of wanting to do the job.

But I want to add here, I was told the first day you go out on your own without a trainer, that they only give you a few hours, and they assume it's going to take you all day; they don't give you an entire route on the first day. That's what I heard, but what truly happens I don't know, and the reason why will be discussed in a later chapter.

So let's get back to the third day I went out with my CCA trainer, who after I told him what I'd done for the first two days, was happy to give me my own hits to deliver so we could both get through the day together.

I had my own scanner and packages to deliver and scan, I had those peach puppies ready to go, and I had two pens, which are a must. I had my postal pouch to carry extra mail in—at least two bundles are in the crook of your arm when carrying out there, but you might use the pouch for a third, depending on your skill. You hold the bundles like a waitress carrying the meatloaf special in a diner.

When we arrived at the first hit on the route, we parked on a typical city street, filled with homes and a few businesses. He hands me the 'hit' and he points to this house on the corner, then begins to go through a little story about how #24 is the side door, 24A is at the back, and the mailbox all alone at the beginning of the driveway is 24 something—I don't even remember now. Now once more, I ask him, "How in God's name would I know all that if I'd never delivered this route before?" He just shrugged because there is no answer for that question. Well, there is one, but you won't like it. The answer is that I wouldn't know any of it, as carriers don't make it a habit of walking around entire perimeters of homes searching for house numbers.

And that takes me off on an entirely new tangent.

House numbers.

Like mailboxes, you never know where those damn numbers might be. They might be on the front door, or on the steps, or on a porch pole, or maybe they're on the mailbox, wherever the fuck that is, or maybe they're above the door, or to the side of it, or better yet: there are two front doors, and each one has a different number, like 26 and 28.

Many times you're going to reach a house and there'll be absolutely no house number. So what do you do? Well, if you just delivered to 30 Rosewood St, the next house has no number, and the one after it is 34 Rosewood, it's a pretty good bet the missing house number is 32. One thing to try, and a lot of the times I got lucky by doing this, is there would be a name on the mailbox, so I could then match the name on the letter for the one on the mailbox, sans house number.

I swear to God, it's like a fucking game show out there! Find the house number for five thousand dollars! I'll spin the wheel for the name Sanchez, Skip. No wait, I'll solve the puzzle! Is it Ruth Jones in house number 20? It is? What did I win? I have to work eleven hours today? And it's raining? And it's thirty-three degrees out? And it's a Headliner day? Wow, Skip, this game sucks.

So have fun playing the house number's game, because it's just as much fun as 'where is the mailbox' game.

Back to my first hit. Where I was basically almost totally alone on this street.

Next the trainer tells me about the house with a thousand apartments, which was something I came across a lot in the city of Everett, where an Irish name on a mailbox was about as rare as a letter carrier leaving his job because he's finished at noontime—don't get the joke yet, believe me, in due time you sure will if you work as a CCA. The terrible part is; it won't be funny then either!

Once the multi-family is explained to me, he tells me where to go next, then do a loop and finish up where I began. Then he jumps into the van and is off to do a hit of his own. When he's done, he'll come back for me and off we'll go to the next hit on the route.

Off I go to the house he just told me about with a dozen different variations of the number 24, and though I was just shown where it all is, I had still never set foot on the property. I figured it out thanks to the explanation, but I still needed to keep my eyes open. Let me explain why: one of the apartments had instructions like this: Go to the back of the house, walk up the stairs to the back deck, and that door is where mail goes. Not that hard right? But before that, I was told: the door you can see from where we're standing is for this number, then over by the back deck there's a mailbox, all alone, that box is for that other number. And all this while you're focusing on the mail in your hand and on the crook of your arm like a waiter carrying a dish full of spaghetti, and trying to get comfortable.

But we're not done yet. Just before he told me all of this, he took about forty pounds of Headliners and put them in my postal pouch which was over my shoulder.

The second the weight hit the bag and I almost fell over onto my side, I said, "Holy shit! How much weight is in here? And I'm supposed to carry this all around the street with me?"

I was told it's not that heavy, that's it about thirty pounds, and he may have been correct. But what he seemed to have forgotten is that he'd been doing the job for twenty years or more. I just started. Christ, give me a chance to build up some tolerance or better yet, let me break up the hits so they're a little smaller on Headliner day.

But I'm training, so I don't get to make these decisions, so I prepared to carry this shit with me though I was beyond miserable.

But here's what happened, and I don't know if it was because I didn't really get proper instructions, or I wasn't hearing it right, or it was a simple miscommunication, but as soon as I finished with that first house and began to walk down the street, where I thought I would deliver, then cross over to the other side of the street and come back, I realized the house numbers were *not* matching up to the mail I had in my hand. I walked to a few houses, the mail bag fucking killing me as it was so heavy, and I re-confirmed that yes, this wasn't the way to go. But here's my dilemma. I had no idea how the numbers ran at all, and as I looked around and across the street, I couldn't figure it out.

Now, if you're on your own and you think you're going to call in to a supervisor for help, you can, but it will be a waste of time. See, they don't know the routes either, as they aren't out there delivering them. So you're going to have to figure it out on your own.

So what did I do? I said fuck it, and I crossed the street and waited for the trainer to return, not a piece of mail delivered other than that first house. While I waited I called another letter carrier I knew and vented to them, which helped me mellow out when the trainer arrived. I take things too seriously: maybe it's a character flaw, maybe it's a benefit. Depends on what situation I'm in I suppose.

When he returned, I told him what had happened and he said no, I was supposed to deliver the first house, *then* cross the street and do a little circle.

Now, I always repeat instructions I'm given back to the person giving them, that way there's no miscommunication. So when I had repeated that I will be going all the way down the street before I crossed over, I got a yes in reply—or I thought I did.

So who was at fault here? Who knows, but all I do know is I was so damn frustrated that I couldn't do a simple task given to me.

Like I said, the concept of delivering mail and parcels is simple, but the actual process put into action is very, very different.

The trainer was an easygoing fellow, and he told me what I was doing wrong. It appears I was supposed to cross the street immediately after delivering to that first house, then do a loop.

So, off I went again to do the hit again.

Now, here's another example of having to read minds.

I get to this building a few minutes later where there are businesses inside. There's this weird-looking structure for mail right on the main path to the front door; it kind of resembles a rectangle on its side with individual rectangle doors the tenant can open on their shelf with their key. I see the place where the Arrow key goes and I use it, the small door opening. I then try to figure out how to unlatch the thing so that the large door will swing open so I have access to the ladder-like shelves for each business.

Think of opening the hood on a car you've never touched before. Sure you know how to do it on your own car, and you know the basic concept, but I'll bet you any amount of money you end up sliding your hand from side to side for a few seconds or longer, as you try to find the latch for that particular model. Why? Because each make and model might be different.

So though I know the damn door should open, I can't figure it out. Finally, one of the tenants comes out, perhaps wondering what that idiot was doing, and he showed me I needed to pull the latch inward. I had been pressing upward. Well, shit, folks, how was I supposed to know what way to do it if I'd never seen this sort of group mailbox in my entire life. Now, the next day I delivered to this place again and it took me seconds to drop mail off and move on to the next address.

Why? Because I'd been there before, if only one time, so now I knew what to do. If only it would always be that way. But it wouldn't, and I knew from the first day I was on my own, I would be doing a different route, and no doubt in a different city, every damn day. It would take months if not years to finally get a general idea of some of the routes I would be tossed on each day. And all of this while it's raining, snowing, both, or the streets and sidewalks are covered in ice and it's ten degrees out. Man, you gotta love New England in the winter time.

The next place I went was another business, this one some kind of rehab place. I had to walk down a small hallway and hand the mail to a woman behind a desk. She was over sixty, and probably in her seventies. Now, here's a pitfall all letter carriers have to watch out for. People think because they're either home or at work but have the time, that you do to. The old woman launched in about her bad knees and blah, blah, blah. I nodded once or twice and said I had to go. Look, I love a good chat, but when delivering mail, there just isn't time, at least not when you're new.

No wait; that would be a lie. The truth was that after how frustrated I felt from not getting to do the hit correctly, I wasn't worrying too much about the time, but I didn't want to hear about an old woman's knees, but later, on the same loop, when I met a tow truck driver who had his garage on that hit, we talked for a few minutes about this and that, and you know what? I felt a whole lot better after that, so to me it was worth it. If you're feeling good, feeling happy, you're going to do a better job, too.

The rest of the day was just one house after another, one multi-family after another.

There was one house I remember however, and what I found funny, in a bad way for letter carriers, is that one of the MSP scans was at this house. MSP scans are placed around the routes you do, usually ten or eleven per route. There are the two important ones; one at the beginning and the last one, which tells someone watching you when you started to deliver and when you finished that last address.

You should scan them all, and you're supposed to have a list when you go out on a route, but whether that happens I can't tell you. It will depend on how good your station is. It should happen, but it might not. But most MSP scans are right there on the front of either the mail boxes of a private residence, or you'll see them on an apartment box that needs an Arrow key. When you use the key, there's the scan bar code. Sometimes though, the MSP barcode is on the side of a mailbox, so if you don't know it's there, how would you know to look?

Hey! There's another game you can play. Where's the fucking MSP scan?

Anyway, back to this house. Picture this: the house is faded white, in disrepair. The cement walkway is degraded, more than an inch missing from the front path. The cement has crumbled to the point it's mostly rubble, the chunks not more than an inch in size. The walkway to the stairs is made up of three cement pieces, the thin line carved into the cement for expansion when it was laid making it easy to see the blocks.

On the small, four by four of a small porch, there's a chair that looks like it belongs in a garbage dump. Trash litters the sidewalk and the path. A slum house in every perceivable way.

Now, I commented to the carrier training me that if it had been snowing, and I was doing that route for the first time, I wouldn't see the inch or more of degraded pathway, nor the rubble and gravel underneath the snow. I would step on the path to go up to the mailbox, and would very likely fall flat on my ass or worse.

But that's not what I found so funny, in an ironic, terrible way.

On that mailbox was an MSP scan. There were multiple ones actually, as over time the others had become so weathered that another needed to be placed there. You mean to tell me, each time someone placed a new MSP scan on that mailbox, not even once did someone decide to flag that house as unsafe? And even if that house isn't getting mail that day, every single day the carrier has to go up that path and climb those stairs to scan the MSP scan.

Whoops, there I go again, preaching about common sense. As someone who believes I have a lot of common sense, once more I wondered if working for USPS might be more of a challenge than I could handle.

I know what you're thinking.

Why didn't I go back to the station and report this house as unsafe and get a Hold put on the mail?

Are you kidding me? You remember what happened last time I tried that? No, this time I did what I should have done the first time. I kept my fucking mouth shut and minded my own business. Hey, you work a job and you're just a peon, you have to know when to simply shut up and do the job and don't worry about what isn't your problem.

You know what? That truly sucks though, and I didn't like having to be forced to act like that one bit. Now, some poor bastard is going to be out there in the snow and they could get seriously hurt because I couldn't do my job and get a Hold placed on that house? Why? Because the people above me were incompetent, that's why.

Ah well, once more, welcome to USPS.

There's one more thing I wanted to add that you should know about when either seeing an unsafe address, such as with a dog, falling ice, ice on the stairs, or a dozen other things. In the end, if you don't feel safe, *don't* deliver to that house. Trust me, the job is not worth you getting hurt, nor should you risk getting hurt so someone can get their Victoria Secret or Crackle Barrel catalog today.

Unless you're delivering life-saving medicine, there's nothing in the mail that can't wait a day or two. And that goes for my own stuff I get delivered to my own address, too. Nothing I have ever gotten couldn't have waited a day or two longer; nothing. Is it nice to get it faster? Sure, but it's not a life or death scenario. It's just mail, folks, don't forget that.

Well, unless it's from Amazon. Then run to get that shit delivered. What do I mean?

That's the next chapter.

Chapter 12
You Work For Amazon.com Now

The holiday season of 2014 was a hell of a time for UPS (the brown trucks). See, UPS had taken on the Amazon contract, promising to deliver millions of packages on time before Christmas.

The problem was, UPS underestimated the sheer volume of parcels that would need to be delivered and unfortunately, they fell woefully short of their promised goals.

Jump to 2015. USPS, the postal service, has been offered the contract, as Amazon wasn't too pleased with UPS. Of course they accepted, seeing dollar signs float past their eyes, like they were in a cartoon.

I can imagine the meeting. "Sure, we can handle a few million more packages a week despite having a quarter the workforce we once did. You want Sunday delivery, too? Hell yes, we can do that. After all, our employees don't need a life, they can work seventy-plus hours a week indefinitely. Will it kill them? Probably, but let's cross that bridge when we come to it. For now, let's only think about the money all the new business is going to take in. We can deal with the logistics of this monumental task later—or maybe never. What was that? You want one day delivery? Ah, well, let me think about it. No, never mind, we can do it. Like I said, our employees don't need Sunday off. I mean, it's not like they work for the post office where there's no Sunday delivery. Hey, Amazon, we got your back."

The frustrating part every employee has to think about on a daily basis while they're running packages like Fed Ex, is that the people who agreed to this will never touch a parcel themselves.

The idea that the people who get to make these decision figured they could just absorb a million packages a year, is utterly ludicrous, but despite this, it's happening right now, if you're going to do this job, it will be you that's living this nightmare every day.

But Sundays are special in their own right, as all you're going to be delivering is Amazon.com packages. It's funny, too, when you're out there, as no one expected Sunday delivery, and most people are pretty surprised when you ring their doorbell to hand them a package.

Many small businesses are closed, so those can't even get their orders delivered on Sunday.

Now, I'm going to let you in on a few little secrets only known to people in USPS when it comes to Amazon.

Though as a carrier you are supposed to scan *Delivered* every single package you deliver to an address, so that the sender had proof of delivery, if for some reason you can't, just make sure you at least always scan the Amazon packages.

Yes, that's right, only worry about the Amazon parcels.

Have to deliver something from Best Buy and one from Amazon and for some reason you have to choose which one gets a scan or can only deliver one? Make sure it's the Amazon one.

I was very surprised to learn that basically all parcels next to Amazon are considered second-rate packages. Yes, that right, USPS has such a hard-on for the Amazon contract, they will gladly let other parcels suffer. Is this because Amazon is demanding a certain level of performance from USPS? Yes probably, but it really sucks when they're striving for perfection with Amazon, and the rest of us who mail parcels with them can go fuck ourselves—our shit can take a little longer if it it's a choice over Amazon.

So let me explain this even another way, as I'm having fun writing this, as the irony is so palpable you have to laugh or you're going to cry.

Let's say you mail your item on a Wednesday, and it arrives at the annex (station) Saturday night, along with a giant group of Amazon parcels. On Sunday, the Amazon stuff will get delivered, but you know where your package is? If you were going to say getting delivered on Sunday as well, you'd be woefully mistaken. Your parcel gets delivered on Monday, as it's not as valuable to USPS to move it on Sunday.

So, basically on Sunday, USPS employees work for Amazon, despite if their paycheck says USPS. I wonder if one day very soon, postal workers will have another patch next to they're post office eagle on their uniforms, one that has a logo of Amazon on it. Yup, a great big letter '**A**' right next to that eagle, but wait; want to bet the eagle will be two inches in size, and the Amazon '**A**' will be four inches?

But we're not done yet with these little nuggets of gold.

Another rule for delivering Amazon packages is to drop that parcel at the address, no matter what.

Here's an example of what I mean.

Let's say there's a gang war going on, or maybe the house is on fire. Either one would be an extreme of course. Now, normally, a letter carrier would see this pretty crazy scenario and decide not to leave that package on the front porch of the house, as it would be considered not a safe place.

Maybe you even have a thief standing in front of the house, with a big sign saying "I'm here to steal the Amazon packages once you leave them!" Now, you'd think the carrier should bring them back, as it's not safe to leave, right? Wrong.

Amazon wants those packages delivered no matter what. They would prefer to have it scanned *Delivered*, and have a customer calling later, whether to complain it was stolen or ask for a replacement, and Amazon would prefer to replace it, then not have it delivered on the day promised.

What? Seriously?

Yes, this is an unwritten policy. Now, when I delivered Amazon packages on Sunday with another 'regular' carrier, he did bring a few parcels back because the businesses were closed and he didn't want to leave the packages on the sidewalk at the front door, but he was really supposed to leave them. But this man had common sense and he did what he knew was right, not what he was told to do.

So remember, as a CCA, if you have to pick and choose what packages to scan, make sure you scan the Amazon packages. You can miss those MSP scans on mailboxes, you can ignore all other scans on packages, such as Priority and First Class, and though someone will talk to you and ask why those scans weren't made later, it won't be the end of the world, but miss those Amazon scans and be prepared for a world of shit.

Now, just before I quit and left USPS employment, another little gem came my way.

It seemed that though UPS (Brown truck), had lost the holiday contract, they were still delivering Amazon packages the rest of the year, though not as much as before. Amazon basically had both UPS and USPS delivering their orders.

Well, at the time of writing this book, Amazon pulled the UPS contract completely and USPS will now solely deliver Amazon packages.

Holy shit! They can't handle what they're doing now.

In fact, to give you an analogy I came up with while working there, you need to be familiar with the novel *Dante's Inferno*.

In the book, the hero has to go through the layers of Hell, where on each level, there are all sorts of ways to make people suffer, such as pushing a boulder up a hill, only to have the boulder reappear at the bottom once it's reached the top. For eternity that poor soul has to push that boulder, only to have to do it again and again each day.

Well, if you work for USPS, welcome to the tenth level of Hell. Here, each morning you will awaken to find a massive, Empire State building pile of Amazon parcels that need to be delivered by the end of the day.

Now, as you can imagine, at the beginning it would be beyond daunting, but as the hours pass the mountain would slowly get smaller, until when the sun finally set, and it would be gone. That's right; every single package has been delivered and scanned. Wow, that was crazy, and it took all you had to get it done. You're now physically and emotionally exhausted.

So you go to sleep, and when you rise the next morning, yup, you guessed it, the mountain is back. But wait; the mountain has doubled in size!

So get to work, because you're going to be doing it six days a week, ten to eleven hours a day for the rest of your life—even most holidays. Or until you make regular and can tell them fuck off, you're not working overtime anymore. But they can still force you to work when they're really short of help and they will.

But look at the bright side. At least no one's whipping you while you deliver the mail for USPS. But I wouldn't put them past them.

One a side note, I wanted to add a few sentences about scans in general and what they really mean. This relates to Amazon deliveries but also any delivery where the parcel or letter needs to be scanned only, no signature.

Let's say I scan a package as 'Delivered' and I hop out of the vehicle and toss it onto the porch. But I was rushing and I didn't read the address of the house properly. The street address was 125 Grove St, but the one I just delivered has an address of 125 Grove Avenue.

According to the scans that will be on record for that parcel, it will say it was delivered at such and such a time. *Proof of delivery* is what that's called.

But here's the catch. It was scanned delivered, yes, but it wasn't delivered to the correct house.

See, the scans only coincide with the zip code of the address, the technology hasn't caught up so that it can prove it was delivered to the exact address on the label, so if you ever don't get something you personally ordered, and when you check tracking information is says it was 'delivered,' but you know you didn't get it, use this little bit of information to make the shipper understand that 'delivered' though a good bet it happened, is not an unconditional guarantee. Signature confirmation is better, in that someone has to sign for it, and more people are seeing the package and reading the address ect.

So scanned *Delivered* does not mean it really was delivered.

Here's another example of that.

The post office offers Next Day delivery. There are two kinds: by noon the next day, and by three in the afternoon.

That means someone mailing an important document pays around twenty dollars to ship it next day. Most get signature confirmation but at times this can be waived by the shipper.

Well, like Amazon parcels, USPS is guaranteeing it will be delivered by these times. But what if the carrier is overloaded and can't get there? Simple, they scan the package as *Attempted* and then get there when they can. Attempted? You're three miles away from the address, and you never drove over there? How the hell did you *attempt* anything? All you did was scan it to stop the clock on the package, which is lying.

Well, apparently USPS either doesn't know or doesn't care that this is unwritten policy. All they care about is the scans, even if what they're basically doing is defrauding their customer by promising something they can't deliver.

I would assume most times a noon delivery date isn't a necessity, and even one o'clock is fine with the receiver, but still, if USPS can't deliver on time, admit it, don't steal from the customers, because that's what they're doing. If you don't get your pizza in under thirty minutes you get it for free if that was the promise when you ordered.

So if you're going to be a CCA, get ready to work every Sunday until you make *regular*, because you will be forced to. The times of being a letter carrier and having Sundays off are long gone. We all know we live in a twenty-four hour world, where even at three in the morning people are buying online. To meet the need, USPS really has no choice in the matter.

Low on manpower and with decades-old equipment, each day they move that mountain, only to have it reappear each morning.

So if you don't like moving mountains, I'd reconsider taking the job as a CCA, but if you like to be overwhelmed, overworked and unappreciated, you'll fit right in.

Chapter 13
My Mailman, My Paperboy

Up until December 2015, the ads (those Headliners I've been talking about all the time) that look like a small newspaper, filled with supermarket circulars and coupons, weren't delivered by USPS.

They were years ago, but then the contract was taken away from USPS and given to some private organization. I know on my street, I would often see a mother pushing a stroller, a child in the stroller, as she went door to door tossing the Headliners onto porches.

They were either wrapped up tight with an elastic, or later, they came in clear plastic bags. These actually were a great hazard for letter carriers. As many people don't take care of their houses or complexes, these Headliners would pile up, left where they were tossed. Add an inch of snow over them, the plastic bag to be more precise, and stepping on one was worse than stepping on ice.

Talk I heard around the station said that this was one of the reasons the private contract was lost and the Headliners were given back to USPS.

Once more, more work has been added to letter carriers, but they're not given a minute of extra time to deliver it. These Headliners arrive at the station on Tuesday or Wednesday, and must be delivered by Saturday. People who get the Boston Globe in my area don't get a Headliner, but everyone else does. What's worse too is that each Headliner has an address on it, so it must be delivered like any other piece of mail.

When I tell you these things suck to deal with, there's really no way I can truly describe just how much. You have to deal with them yourself.

On any given day you have more than enough to carry. Most of the time you have three bundles to deal with. The first two bundles are the letter and flat mail that comes in already sorted from machines. Those are called FSS and DPS, and then you have that other bundle of mail you sorted personally when throwing mail in the morning. Most carriers throw the Headliners with the miss-sorted mail to make it one single bundle.

So what you end up getting is two massive bundles. An easier way is to ignore the designated hits on your route and make up your own, smaller hits, otherwise you'll be carrying fifty pounds of Headliners all day.

But before I go further, I really want to at least try to explain how much these Headliners suck.

First, the paper within is mostly very thin, and there are two dozen or more individual ads. The coupons you get in a newspaper on Sunday are in there, too. Those are even smaller than the rest of the ads. The outer wrapping is like a folder, the paper also thin, but usually larger than the rest of the interior. Almost all the paper of each ad is glossy, so it slips and slides within the paper folder. It's about the size of a daily newspaper, only it's a slippery mess that will not stay together. And you have to deliver a few hundred of these each week, depending on how large your route is. If you have an apartment building or a complex, you can take an elastic and wrap all the Headliners for that one address. Those are easy. Just walk into the building and plop them down on the floor by the mailboxes. Later in the week, after sufficient time has passed, the custodian of that building will come by and toss all those Headliners into the recycle bin.

Yes, you are mostly delivering these for absolutely no reason. I'm sure there are a few people who might look at them, but if I had to guess, I would say ten out of a hundred people want to receive Headliners. You'll see this for yourself when you deliver to homes and the Headliners you left two weeks ago are still on the porch. See, many people see junk mail and don't want it, and they simply toss it to the side, forgotten.

This can be a problem with full mailboxes. It's the customer's job to empty their mailbox and some of these mailboxes could fit three letters at a time. Seriously, they are super tiny. So slide a Headliner into the box and that pretty much does it.

When I delivered Headliners, I mostly tossed them between the screen door or placed them on the porch and used a corner of the mat if one was there to prevent the papers from blowing. I mentioned this in a previous chapter but now will go into more detail.

Remember how I told you about those tiny mail slots in doors barely large enough to fit a standard envelope? Well, you can try, but good luck fitting Headliners through there. Even if you did, the papers are going to fall apart when they land, making one hell of a mess. Don't waste your time. Just toss them between the screen door, or if the mailbox is big enough, put them in there. It would be nice if each one could be rolled up and have an elastic, then delivered that way, but with an address on them, it's harder to do that. The truly annoying part of it all, is that nine out of ten addressed on the routes I delivered got them, so the whole address thing became mute.

Then there are the multi-families, who never clean their mailboxes out and never, and I mean never, bother dealing with the Headliners. For these I barely cared who got what as far as apartment A, B or C. You can do it how you want, but I knew from day one of delivering these that it would be a waste of time; no one cared about them—especially the customers. These are junk mail in the worst way ever.

You know, when the contract was taken by that private company years ago, letter carriers sighed with relief and were told they would never have to deal with them again.

And here they are, back from the past to give every mailman a sore back.

But these Headliners are even more of a headache for CCAs and I'll tell you why.

As a CCA, you'll be delivering a different route each day. So that means every Wednesday through Saturday, your work load will double, if not triple.

See, these Headliners come like newspapers, in bundles, and every carrier should take at least four bundles a day to have it all delivered by Saturday.

But what happens when you arrive on Saturday and no one has taken any Headliners on that route, as both of the other CCAs said screw it? See, the station I worked at was so chaotic, no one was watching what anyone was doing. Like I said, the place seemed to really run on autopilot. If the carriers did their scans, mostly no one was checking up on anyone. Nor do they need to be. All the regular carriers I met at the station and the ones I know personally are pros, who know how to do their job backwards and forwards.

So as I delivered Headliners my first week, I imagined coming in on a Saturday and seeing the entire stack of these there. Now I have to do it all, and when I go and complain to a supervisor that the other carriers had fucked me over, you know what my reply would be?

Well, unless you just began reading this book at this chapter, I think you know.

They wouldn't care, and would tell me to do my job.

Yeah, so I was already filing this shit away for my decision to stay or not. Pros or cons? Which do you think I placed Headliners in?

So the Thursday I started as a CCA was the first week USPS was delivering these things. Oh, lucky me. As I went out and delivered them it was truly terrible, my only bit of luck being that it was a nice day out. It was cold, but the sun was shining and there was no snow on the ground, which was rare for January around Boston.

But as I went house to house, I imagined doing the job three days out of the week with Headliners; while it was snowing, raining, windy, or all of the above.

And I wasn't too pleased with how I imagined that all playing out.

Maybe if I began the job in the Spring, where on top of the massive work load, at least the weather outside would have been milder, but I began in January, in the heart of winter. Seriously? What the fuck was I thinking?

There's a reason why seven out of ten new CCAs quit in under a month.

So if you don't mind being a glorified paperboy and dealing with Headliners Wednesday through Saturday, basically delivering a newspaper to over ninety percent of the addresses on your route, and while doing this, still have to deal with letters, magazine and packages, then you're tougher than I am and I wish you luck.

Two more chapters to go, then you can toss this book into the recycle bin.

Chapter 14
Audits

Though this part of delivering mail wasn't something I dealt with personally, but in the spirit of full disclosure, I wanted to add it simply because I find it amusing.

An audit is when personnel come from a head office and they walk the route with you. They do this to see how much time you're using to deliver the route. See, the route is set up by those hits, and perhaps the time you have is more than you need, and if so, then the auditor would make a recommendation for your route to have a street or two added to it—or maybe another large apartment building.

Basically, the auditor is with you the entire day, simply following you as you do your job. Annoying? Of course it is, but even though it might be, can you see why they would do this. I'm sure there are a few routes that could get a little added to them, but I bet you they're most definitely *few* in number.

See, when you're out there delivering, you need to take into account things the auditor won't be dealing with. First, they won't come out on a raining, or snowy day, nor will they come out if there's ice on the ground.

In fact, they usually pick a very nice day, when you can walk faster and your route is easier. See, even if your route does have some extra time on it each day, the second you get bad weather, you're going to be going slower, and you're going to need that extra time, so that's why a regular carrier does not 'run' his route, even when the weather is nice. Slow and steady, don't rush. Can you imagine walking a route in the snow? Most people don't shovel, ice everywhere. It really needs to be experienced for oneself to truly appreciate how absolutely terrible it is, but on these days, which come frequently in New England, there's no such thing as 'extra' time.

So of course, they only audit on good days because they're basically trying to fuck you over, as a letter carrier. They don't care how much you have to work, and their job is to add more on top of what you have if they can prove it feasible.

So don't be surprised if the days you get audited are 'light mail' days. Or days when mail is actually held back so you don't have too much.

But the funny thing about that holding back mail is that nowadays, with Amazon burying USPS in packages, they simply can't do it. The mail needs to be kept moving or else everyone will be buried.

So you know what? Since Amazon's contract, there have been no legitimate audits.

That's right, none.

If you haven't figured out the reason, I will state it here clearly.

With the mail so heavy, and everyone overloaded, if they did an audit now, the result would be that streets would need to be *removed* from a route, as it would be discovered that the letter carriers didn't have sufficient time. So to avoid this, as taking away streets is the last thing they want to do, is that no full audits have happened in a very long time.

None of this matters to people who are just postal customers, but if you're a letter carrier, believe me, this shit matters and nothing is more frustrating than having some pencil pusher follow you around and try and tell you how to deliver mail, especially when other than the audits on a nice day, the people telling you never leave the office.

And I have heard stories about what they do. One was when a carrier wanted to go use the bathroom for his ten minute break, and the auditor wanted the carrier to wait and finish a street before he left so he could be more productive. The carrier had been on that route for years, and knew what he was doing.

Letter carriers have enough to do daily without dealing with this crap for a day. But like I stated above, nowadays, no audits are taking place because if they were, the people making them wouldn't like what was discovered.

And you can't take streets away if there's nowhere to add them later, and you can't create new routes if there are no people to deliver them, as they're so short of help.

Chapter 15
Sunday Delivery

Okay, so we're nearing the ending of my employment with USPS as a CCA. So far, I hope you've found the tale either amusing, enlightening, or downright shocking, depending on your point of view.

So let's do a recap before moving into my last day on the job.

The first week was pretty easy, as it was nothing but classroom time, and other than fighting boredom and sleep, the week was mostly painless.

The second week was different.

The work week at USPS begins on a Saturday, and that day I did my LLV training, which was driving around on an obstacle course for six hours or more. Sunday I had the day off, but I'm going to let you in on a little secret of why I had that Sunday off.

Even before I did the LLV training, I was supposed to call the annex and let them know I was assigned there. But I had a feeling if I did, I would immediately be told to come in, and either move packages or be a jumper for Amazon deliveries. And frankly, I wasn't ready to give up my life just yet. See, as I said, I knew what I was getting into, or at least I thought I did. But though I knew the logistics of it, I found out to implement them was a far cry from what I first believed.

I also felt that working for what is basically a soulless corporation, where no matter how hard I work—or don't—as the case may be, would matter little in the grand scheme of things. For you only get a raise if it's in the Union contract, and when that happens, everyone gets a raise, no matter how exceptional or worthless they are. If they're employed, they get that raise.

Me, personally, I like to work where I'm appreciated as a person, not just another number filling a slot. Of course, this doesn't matter to a lot of people, and if you're like that, and all you need is a paycheck, then by all means, try this job. Hey, you have nothing to lose by trying.

And who knows, you might get stationed somewhere that the management makes you feel like you're part of a team, and not just another drone. It can happen, despite my misfortune.

But back to the rundown.

So I had Sunday off, and on Monday, due to a holiday on Friday, I needed to do one more day of Orientation. Then on Tuesday, after calling Monday afternoon when I was finished for the day at class, I reported at the annex for training.

Tuesday and Wednesday I worked with the first OJT trainer, Tim, who was a pleasure to work with and I learned a lot. It was still a long ass day though. Once the route was finished, Tim was assigned overtime to do *collections,* which is driving around after five o'clock and picking up mail at the blue mailboxes on city streets. Of course, I have nothing to do here and I basically just sat in the passenger seat while he did his thing. Not bad with the exception I would have preferred being done for the day. Plus, I'm a person who suffers from motion sickness, so put me on a boat or in a car that I'm not driving and I get sick as a dog. So no, I wasn't enjoying driving around while Tim did his thing, but I had no choice. We were in another city and he was my ride back to the station.

So both days I worked from 7:30 in the morning until six that night.

Long days for someone who until that point was working from home. For those two days I walked a lot of miles, too, and I wasn't someone who walked a lot normally. Frankly I hate walking, so to pick this as a profession was kind of stupid.

Still, it was a challenge and I wanted to see if I could do it. I knew I could quit at anytime, so the pressure of really needing the job to pay the rent wasn't on my back. I was there because I chose to be there, not because I had no choice. One less bit of stress with that. No one likes to be in a job they truly hate but due to financial issues have to stay there.

So for those two days I worked ten hours or so, and let me tell you, I slept like a baby those two nights.

On Thursday I had a different trainer, and once more worked ten hours, this time getting a taste of actually delivering.

But still, though I had a handle on what I was doing with the OJT, and it was vastly different than if I was on my own. I mean, the trainer would hand me the 'hit' and point to where I had to begin. If I'd been alone, I would have had no idea where to begin. They make it sound like it's so easy to know where to go, but I'm telling you now; they're full of shit!

If you haven't delivered the route before, and you have never gone door to door on that particular route for some reason—like you're a Jehovah's Witness in your spare time—you're in for a lot of walking around in circles trying to figure out where it all is.

Friday was my second day with the same trainer from Thursday and this time at least the day went smoother. I 'threw' the mail myself and got my second taste of Headliners. We also did some the previous day as well.

But for most of the day I was informed I would be going back to the office around two to be used to sort packages, but when two o'clock finally came, my trainer didn't want to let me go, as he didn't want to be out all night delivering the route, as I slowed him down immensely. Around three, he was told by the station not to bother bringing me back, and I stayed on the route until we finished.

But, when we were heading back at around four in the afternoon, I had no idea if I was off or not. Let me tell you; that feeling sucks. You've just worked eight hours and for all you know, you're going to be working for another two or three. You have no say in it, you will do it or if you don't want to, you're only option is to quit.

Not a pleasant feeling. Especially when it's pitch dark outside and you might get sent out to a route you don't know to deliver streets you've never seen before, and do it all in either inclement weather, in the dark, or both.

But I wasn't needed and I was allowed to go home after an eight hour day. If you work as a CCA and later as a regular carrier, you'll quickly find out that an eight hour day will feel like half a day.

That Saturday I had off, and after working about fifty-five hours, most of it outside walking around in the cold, climbing stairs ect, I enjoyed that day off immensely. I will admit I didn't even think I had that week in me. Though not a complete couch potato, when you don't have a job that's physically demanding, to then get thrown into a job like CCA is pretty taxing for a lot of people, especially if you're in your forties and can't bounce back like when you were in your twenties. Getting old sucks!

I want to point out that the entire week I trained it was nice weather. Cold, but no rain or snow—which is probably why I lasted even for one week.

But days off never go slow and I had to work Sunday for Amazon, oh wait, sorry, I meant USPS. I kept getting them mixed up.

The weather on Sunday was horrible, I mean truly horrible. The wind was blowing and it was raining sideways. That day alone the Boston area received three to four inches of rain, which caused flooding and all sorts of messes.

To step out in the rain meant you were soaked within ten seconds or less. It was truly one of the worst rainstorms any state can get.

And it was the first taste of actual bad weather I got to experience.

The funny part is I wasn't out there walking around in it. I was the jumper in a van delivering Amazon packages with a regular carrier who was working overtime. Overtime isn't bad if you're a regular carrier. The ones who have been in for over twenty years make around twenty-five dollars an hour or so, so when it becomes time and half as well, it's good pay for what you're doing. But if you're me and you're getting sixteen dollars an hour….well, let's just say I kept thinking I could get a job at Target or Stop and Shop, work less hours and make ten bucks an hour and mostly be inside, with the exception of having to be the guy who gets the shopping carts from the parking lot.

I reported for work at ten in the morning, and I found the place was bustling. There were CCAs from all over the district there. I met people from my Orientation class that were stationed all over the cities around Boston, and I was surprised to see them at my annex on Sunday. There had to be at least fifty drivers and jumpers there.

The Amazon packages weren't ready yet for us though, due to the planes and trucks coming in late because of the weather. Planes can't fly in bad weather, I mean really bad weather, so no doubt there were delays. So at least an hour was spent simply waiting around.

Then, to my surprise and disappointment, the douche bag of a manager was there, and he called everyone into a large room to give us a safety talk. Once more, his talk was more of him pontificating, and him telling stories that really are too long and boring to be interesting, but like I said, this is a guy who likes captive audiences.

Once more I was thinking why the hell is this guy here? Normally, from everything I knew of the annexes, supervisors run things. This manager never should have been there, especially on a Sunday. Still, if he wasn't talking to me, then so be it, but having a dislike of the guy, I wasn't pleased to see him, as I'm sure others felt the same from all I'd heard previously.

When he was finished with his safety talk, where he once more made sure to inform all the new people there that if they hurt their hand or something else was hurt in some minor way, don't bother filing an accident report, as it was a lot of paperwork for his office to deal with.

Can you say 'asshole,' because that's what I was thinking once more. Sharing this tidbit with some regular letter carriers I know from a different station later, and a few other items worth mentioning for drama's sake, one carrier replied, "What a douche bag," which is where I got that name here for the manager.

Once I was released from the meeting with everyone else, it was time to wait some more. I met a new CCA who had been a carrier for about a year and a few months and she informed me she was making regular in another two weeks. So what they said about people making regular faster than before is true. But remember, Chelsea is a massive annex, one of the biggest in the state, so once more, you would move up there faster than if you're assigned a smaller annex with less people. There it could be years before you make regular; and during all that time, no benefits, no sick days, nothing.

As a matter of fact, as a CCA, you only can work 360 days in a row; including days off. So on your 361st day, you get a five day vacation. Then you're basically rehired for paperwork's sake for the next 360. But, if for any reason they forget to do this, don't say anything, because if you show up for work on day 361, work it, and when you come in the next day, let them know, and according to Union rules, they have to make you a regular carrier. Years ago, they had a position called *casual,* where people were hired for ninety days at a time, then fired and rehired. A carrier told me of someone who after ninety days, wasn't laid off, and still came in to work. On day ninety one that person became a full time employee, with benefits ect. So it happens.

I would have gotten my five days mandatory off right at Christmas time, which would have been great for me but would have been frustrating for supervisors who needed bodies desperately.

Anyway, back to rainy Sunday.

When I left Friday, I forgot to give back the Arrow key I had signed out. One reason was when I returned to the office at four, I didn't do the regular things you do when you return from a route, so I was thrown out of the little repetition I'd done for the past few days. When I arrived home and found out I still had the Arrow key on me, technically I was supposed to go back and return it. But two things made me not do this. One was I knew they were a spare set as I was training, and two, was that I didn't want to go back. I'd had enough and if I got in trouble when I give them back later—I'll be honest here—I really didn't give a shit. I mean, it's not like they were going to fire me for bringing them home.

Besides, as a new CCA, don't be afraid to play dumb. Just say, "Gee. I didn't know I had to call to let you know," or "Gee, I didn't even realize until I came in this morning I still had them. I'm so sorry." All they're going to say is don't do it again.

I didn't call and tell them on the chance they told me I had to bring them back, so in this case, I went with the saying, 'better to ask for forgiveness over permission.'

At around eleven-thirty in the morning or so it was finally time to go out in the maelstrom of a day and deliver Amazon packages.

The driver I was with was a new guy to me, someone I hadn't worked with before. He'd been a letter carrier for about thirty years. He was a pleasure to work with and though it was a terrible day due to the weather, at least when you have a nice person as your partner the day goes smoother.

We had ninety-seven packages to deliver in the city of Everett, Ma., which is a good-sized city.

There's a loading dock where the vehicles can be backed up so that carriers can load their trucks with an overhang to keep them out of the rain—the packages, too.

We didn't use this. Instead, he pushed the bins out into the rain and loaded them there. We had three bins worth of packages. When I was pushing an empty bin back into the station, I noticed a private car parked in one of the slips at the loading dock, which meant one postal vehicle had to load in the rain and not at the dock. I asked why that personal car was there and I was told it was probably one of the clerks that had come in early, around three in the morning.

Now, like I said before, I think too much, and my first thought was why didn't some supervisor or even that pompous manager, see that private car there and have the clerk move it, as that space was for the carriers to load up in. Sure, at three in the morning it was fine, but have the owner move it later, or better yet, don't park there at all.

So we had to load our packages in the downpour because some lazy clerk didn't want to get wet when walking from their car into the building. Just one more case of a poorly-managed station, and lucky me, I was now part of it.

Because I was delivering in Everett, and the Arrow key was from the same city, I kept the key for that day too in case I needed it when I asked about returning it when I arrived that day. See, sometimes there's a small square trap door about four inches in diameter with a lock that needs an Arrow key. Open that little door and there will be a key to enter that building. Don't forget after unlocking the door, and use your foot to keep it open, to put the key back, or the next CCA or mailman won't be able to get inside.

All the packages were soon loaded, the carrier having done this in a certain order—see, each parcel has a number written on it by a clerk, and that number corresponds with directions, turn by turn, so that you go from one delivery point to the next.

But be careful; sometimes directions say do a U-turn, and if you did, it would probably get you killed. Use the directions with discretion.

Then it was time to head out, and I wasn't looking forward to it. When I'd left that morning the rain hadn't been falling too hard so I'd decided I didn't need rain gear, but a normal winter coat. Man, that was a big mistake. As soon as I left, the rain became a monsoon.

Once more, before we headed out, it was time to hit the bathroom to make sure we would be good for a while once on the street. Once that task was finished and I was walking out to the van, I couldn't believe my bad luck as the manager was walking right past me.

Crossing my fingers this asshole didn't want to say anything to me, I kept my head low and kept walking, but no sooner did I reach him then he says, "Be safe out there."

"Oh," I thought, "Maybe this guy isn't so bad after all, and it's myself who's the asshole here."

Now, before I tell you the rest, I need to reiterate on a little secret that all regular carriers use when being told something or being forced to complete a task it's possible to get done, given the amount of time to complete it. Because believe me, supervisors will push you and make you want to run the routes or else you risk listening to them give you grief. Let them; don't ever run around like an idiot for a supervisor, not if you're smart. Do your job and be productive but don't 'run' the route for fear of listening to them. Their job is to get the mail delivered with minimal manpower, so they will push you till you can't take it anymore if you let them.

When a supervisor tells you to do three hours worth of a hit in two hours, don't argue, don't fight with them, just simply say, "Okay, I'll do my best."

Let's mull that over for a moment, shall we?

"I'll do my best."

Not, "I'll get it done."

Or, "I'll make it happen."

You say, "I'll do my best."

Because that's all you can really do. To promise anything else would be putting yourself into a position you might have to explain later, and if given an impossible task, to then say you'll do it would make you a liar.

So what do you say when given a task, no matter what it is? You say, come on now, say it with me, "I'll do my best."

Because in the end, that's all any of us can do given any situation.

So when I was told to be safe out there, and because I knew this from all my friends who are carriers, I instinctively replied, "I'll do my best." Which once more, given the environment I was heading off into, was all I could say as a reply without promising something I couldn't commit to.

Well, the manager shouldn't have said anything, he should have left it at that, but no, not this guy. And once more, he we go again.

He said, "Uh-uh, wait a second, come back here."

I stopped walking and rolled my eyes as I turned around to see what the hell he could possibly want. He waved me closer, so I did.

"We don't use that term here," he said.

Once more I was speechless, which for me is a rarity. I said nothing, waiting, which with this guy, wasn't long at all.

"I don't like that," he continued.

"Oh, okay," I said, not believing this and I admit, being a little patronizing to him.

He then said, "No, not okay."

"Then what am I supposed to say?" I asked.

"You say 'I will be,' " he explained. As in, 'I will be safe out there.'

Yeah, I wasn't going to say that, as I would be promising something I couldn't commit to. So I said nothing. Just stood there and looked at him.

"And by the way," he began, "the other day when you had an issue with that Hold you did this and that and…"

I'm not going to continue the rest as it would be tedious for you to read, and I want you to be entertained. Needless to say, he rehashed all that piece of drama about the house with the broken stair. This time I rebutted a few times, not just taking it, but once more I realized arguing with this guy wasn't worth my time, so eventually he got bored and the conversation was over—which was fine by me.

So as I was walking away he repeated, "Don't forget to be careful out there."

I was at the swinging doors that led out to the loading dock when he said this and I stopped and opened my mouth, but the words he expected me to say weren't coming out—ever—so I said,

"Uh, I don't know how to reply to that," which was my quiet little way of stating that I refuse to say what you want me to.

And how dare he? Who the hell does he think he is actually telling employees what they must say?

Once more he said, "I'll be safe."

I simply turned around and pushed through the swinging doors, feeling once more pretty damn aggravated. And now I had to go work for five hours feeling like I'm working for someone who was a real jerk. The guy had that effect on me, basically putting me in a bad mood the second I saw him.

Have you ever gotten the creepy-crawlies when someone you disliked entered the room, and if you even had to spend a minute in that room with them you'd think you'd go crazy? Yeah, that's the effect this guy had on me, which sucks when it's your boss and the guy is always under foot, like a cat that's desperate for love, or in this guy's case, looking for attention.

Of course, the torrential downpour didn't make my mood any better, nor if I had to guess, anyone else who was delivering that day.

An important thing I need to return back to is that I suffer from motion sickness. So to be in a job for the entire week where I was always the passenger was for me, asking for trouble.

No one wants to go to work every day feeling nauseous, and if you did, I bet you'd quit pretty fast. When I look back to that week, I realize I should have taken Dramamine before each day, but as I assumed I was going to have my own truck, I wasn't thinking about a week of training where I was a passenger all the time.

And one thing I have to admit, is that all the trainers drove around pretty roughly, taking corners much to fast, hitting the brakes hard. Look, I get it; a lot of people don't think about passengers when they're driving, so they drive the same way they do when alone, which basically means they're rougher than they should be.

That meant for the entire week, I was nauseous a lot of the time, which really became unbearable.

And Sunday was the worst of them all. Assigned to be the jumper all day, all me and the driver did was drive around, constantly stopping and starting. It took quiet a toll on me.

The work itself on a Sunday is pretty painless, and if it had been a relatively normal day it would have been simple, but it wasn't a normal day, it was raining heavier than it had for a long time.

It was so bad out that one house almost didn't get their packages because the entire street was flooded. Two by fours were floating around in the water it was so deep. But I was able to walk up to the edge of the floodwater, and by going into a driveway next door to the assigned house, I tossed the two packages over the railing where they landed near the door. The front steps were completely flooded, as was the sidewalk, so if not for this, that house wouldn't have received their Amazon order till Monday, which in Amazon's eyes seems to be the end of the world for some reason.

So for the next four hours I sat in the passenger seat, jumping out when a house was on my side, and the driver delivering a package if the house was on his side. This carrier, like the others I'd met, didn't seem to ever want to stop and take a break, not even for five minutes. So though I had taken a sandwich, there was literally no time to eat it. Luckily, I'd taken two apples as well, and when hunger became unbearable, I would quickly eat an apple in under a minute.

After a week of this, I admit I was getting tired of having my lunch break given to me as if it was a favor. See, for every eight hours you work, you get two ten minute breaks, and a half hour for lunch. USPS is going to deduct that half hour for lunch if you work over six hours, whether you like it or not, so shit, you might as well take it.

But none of the carriers I worked with took any form of a lunch and I had to constantly ask for a break. Look, I'm not five-years-old, I shouldn't have to ask to take a lunch, or use the bathroom, ect. Sure, when I was out on my own I could then dictate when I wanted to take a break, but for the week I was in, I really got fed up with it. Add that to Sunday being a horror show weather wise, and then tack on being car sick, and you know what you get?

Someone who'd have enough of this shit and decided that was it.

See, as we were driving around in the rain, I was going over everything in my head that would entail the job I was going to be doing alone in another day or so.

I didn't like what I came up with either.

Let's add it all up and break it down.

1: The manager I worked for was an asshole, someone you would never want to go to if you were having an issue.

2: Yes, there is a Union there, but the station was such a mess that I sure wasn't looking forward to ever needing them.

3: Back to the station being total chaos, so I never knew who the hell was in charge, what supervisor to talk to, or where to go at any given time.

4: Which brings us to here, which is that I didn't feel I was getting enough training for the monumental job of doing a new route every damn day.

5: There was no one to ask. Once training is done, you're on your own. You can't have a carrier come over and help you, because they have their own routes to set up. Ask a supervisor? Hell no. They know nothing about setting up individual routes; they will be absolutely no help at all.

6: Headliners. Every Wednesday through Saturday I would have to deal with these pains in the ass, and if the previous carrier on the route I'm doing say on Friday, didn't bother to take any Headliners on Thursday, guess who ends up taking more than their share? If you think I'm whining, then I hope you take the job, and after a month of getting fucked on Saturday, when the Headliners MUST be delivered, and no one else has bothered to do any the prior days, and now your workload is double or triple, though you get the same pay, then come back and let's talk about this part again.

7. After getting to deliver on a few routes, and seeing how ridiculous it is to find mailboxes, addresses, and names, the idea of having to do a new route every bloody day was simply not worth it to me.

8. You'll be expected, without question, to work six days a week, a minimum of sixty hours per week, if not more. You have no say in this, your only option if you can't handle it is to start calling in sick. But on the first day you come back to the office at six o'clock, and they tell you to go back out for another two hours and you can't, you have something important planned, like your kid's recital, your only choice is to go back out again or quit.

Many CCAs have done this I've heard. One CCA came back to the station in Cambridge, Ma. He finished and was done at 7:30 P.M., so he'd been on the clock since seven that morning. He was told he needed to go out again for two more hours upon coming back. For him that was the last straw and he said he quit and left.

I have heard stories, though extreme, where CCAs just left their LLVs in the street with the ignition keys in them, then quit and went home. Hey, I hoped they curbed and parked it before they quit.

Back to the list.

9: Zero communication between employees and management, or at least that's what I saw and felt. For all I know it wasn't like that, but shit, this is about me and how I saw my future workplace.

10: It's New England in January. For sixteen bucks an hour it's not worth getting rained on, snowed on, or all of the above, not when Headliners are added, and doing a new route each day so that you're walking around in circles, with no one to ask for help. Think I'm full of shit? Then when you're out there, lost, go ahead and call in to the office, see what kind of assistance you get.

11: Though paper maps are supposed to be supplied when you do a new route, and I made sure to double and triple check this information, none are provided; they expect you to use your cell phone. My cell phone is small and not for that kind of thing. If I need to find someplace, I do research before I go, but not knowing day to day where I'd be, there was no possibility of doing research the previous day at home and printing out what was needed.

Finally all the packages were delivered and we were heading back to the office at around four in the evening, but I had no way of knowing if I was truly finished, for I could have returned and been told I had to go out for another three hours.

That wouldn't have happened even if I was told to however, as I'd decided to quit once I returned that day.

As a matter of fact, as I returned to the station at four, and I was walking past a few carriers who were standing near an overflowing bin full of Amazon packages that were going out to be delivered, I asked them and they confirmed this. So some of those guys were heading out at four in the evening on a Sunday to deliver for a few more hours.

Meanwhile, a female supervisor who had just finished telling the carriers to go deliver them, walked away while saying, "I'm so sick of all the moaning and crocodile tears from those guys."

Wow, have much empathy for your employees?

I asked around and was told this particular supervisor wasn't a screw-up as a letter carrier and actually had been doing such a good job that she'd been recruited to be a supervisor. She told me a few minutes later she worked an average of eighty hours a week.

Wow, yes I was impressed, but what I also saw was one of those workaholics, who because they don't mind working a billion hours a week, they don't see why everyone else can't do it, too. So this is someone who could care less if you're on hour eleven and don't want to go out again that day.

So that was it for me. Maybe it was because I was soaking wet and nauseous, and had worked about fifty-six hours, all outside, the previous week and I wasn't used to it, and was totally exhausted, but that was when I decided I didn't want to do the job for another damn second.

But I hadn't officially quit yet and I found what happened next amusing.

When I went to give that supervisor my Arrow key, she asked where I'd gotten it from. I told her I'd had it since Friday. Well, she frowned and was about to give me some gentle discipline on how I was supposed to call and report that I'd taken the key home, but before she could get started, I told her politely to hold that thought, in a second it wouldn't matter.

She didn't understand and wanted to continue so I asked her again. "Trust me," I said. "In a minute the Arrow key won't matter at all." Besides, if the person in the cage had done their job, why wasn't it noted that the Arrow key had not been returned? Sure, it's good to have CCAs who are responsible, but what's the point of signing the key out if no one will ever check if it's missing? Like I said, the station was a mess, and seemed to run on autopilot. Even If I'd commented on this, it wouldn't have been well received.

Then I said the job wasn't for me, and once more commented on how absolutely amazing the letter carriers that do this job every day are, and I will never look at a CCA or any mail carrier the same way again.

Nor should you.

There are a lot of jobs out there a person can work, but I truly can't imagine more than a handful that would be considered as tough to do on a daily basis as being a letter carrier. And now, with the Amazon contract, constant scans on practically every piece of mail other than First Class, bulk and flat mail, Headliners every week, and God only knows what the higher-ups will throw at the letter carriers next week—because at the end of the day, shit rolls down hill and the letter carriers are expected to simply deal with whatever is thrown at them, regardless if it's possible or not—the job will only become more difficult as the years go by.

I'm going to repeat the saying about how you don't know a man until you've walked a mile in his shoes, and the saying goes double for being a mail carrier. Well, I walked more than a mile in their shoes, I did it for an entire week, and still, didn't touch on the full scope of the job in it's entirely. But it was enough for me, and if I could go back in time, I would never have even tried—will note here I was pretty damn sure I wasn't up to the task to begin with, so it's not like I was all macho, strutting in there and saying the job was easy.

So I'm going to say now what every damn person in America should be telling their letter carrier. I'm talking to any carrier who is reading this now.

"Thank you for doing what you do."

It's true your job gets no appreciation, and it's because everyone takes you for granted, but I won't ever again.

Unfortunately, there's no way to get every citizen in America to do your job for a week, so they can truly understand the monumental undertaking you all do on a daily basis.

Without you out there each day, USPS would crumble, much the same as it did during the strike of 1970. You keep the country moving, even if the average person doesn't even realize it.

You're the unsung heroes of America, right along side the Ironworkers, garbage men and all the other jobs we as a country rely on but most people never think twice about, of the people who do them day after day.

I walked a mile in your shoes and I was found wanting, but though I wasn't able to do it, at least now, there's one more person out there in the world who understands what you do, and has nothing but respect for what it takes.

In conclusion, the mail doesn't get to your house by magic, it gets there thanks to the hardworking men and women of the Untied States Postal Service, and if there's one thing I took with me after my experience, it's having the knowledge to write this book, so that hopefully, others can see what the job truly entails, and by simply reading this book, can also give mail carriers everywhere the respect and admiration they so richly deserve.